ANDY BRIGGS

D1502118

OPEN ROAD

INTEGRATED MEDIA

Dad, I know you're going to love this one . . .

1

The snap of a branch underfoot sounded like a gunshot in Samson's ears. He froze, partly concerned that shifting his bodyweight might break another rotting branch, partly because he didn't want to alarm his prey.

He held his breath. The humid rainforest air formed beads of perspiration that rolled down his dark brow, stinging his eyes. He wiped them away with a muddy sweatband wrapped on the wrist of the same hand with which he gripped the razor-sharp machete.

The discordant caws of African gray parrots, the mindless chitter from flocks of Sharpe's starlings, and the blood pumping in his ears filled his senses. Behind, his two companions had frozen too. They stared at him with a mixture of tension and anger at his loud clumsy steps. One was Jean-Paul, his face heavily pockmarked from birth, who was weighed down by the large hemp-net strung across his back. The other, Nicolas, gripped a shotgun—his clothes, like those of the others, were dirty and stained with dried sweat and blood, but his weapon was meticulously maintained. They looked the part with their bandannas, cropped hair, and crooked teeth. There was never any humor in their faces; theirs were lives spent in the dark corruption of human misery. Here, in the untouched verdant jungle, they were unwelcome intruders.

For them the rainforest held no wonder. The velvet mist hugging the mountainside was an irritant, thorny plants and infernal insects a problem they would prefer to burn away. But this was where their quarry lived.

A loud crack made Samson narrow his eyes to sharpen his vision against the shafts of sunlight that pierced the canopy. Another snap confirmed something was moving. Something big. He scanned the dense foliage until he spotted movement. Through the gaps in the branches he saw a huge black shape slowly cross.

Samson ducked, thankful they had approached downwind and their presence remained undetected. For a moment, he lost track of the beast—then a huge black hand, twice the size of his own, but equally dexterous, reached out and effortlessly snapped a slender bamboo stem. The cleared vegetation gave Samson a full view of the 260-pound mountain gorilla.

Shaggy black fur covered the ape but its hand was hairless, picking at the stems with exquisite care. Samson wasn't interested in its remarkable similarity to a human hand—a pair of gorilla hands brought $200 on the black market, bought by the superstitious to bring good luck and fertility. They could sell the bushmeat to local towns for a pretty profit. If they could capture a baby alive, then that could bring a payday from $5,000 upward. Poaching endangered species was a lucrative sideline for Samson, away from his rebel activities for the notorious Forces démocratiques de libération du Rwanda.

Long white canine teeth, in better condition than Samson's own, stripped the bamboo. Intelligent brown eyes peered from under the gorilla's low brow.

Samson only saw the creatures as a means to a financial end. He had no love for them. Nor was he concerned that there were less than a thousand mountain gorillas left in the wild. By the end of the day, there would be fewer by his hand.

The female reached for another stem and the undergrowth moved as more of her band emerged. Samson could make out another two females and three juveniles no bigger than two-year-old humans. The youngsters were chasing one another up trunks and then hanging precariously from branches before cannonballing into the ferns.

With one hand, Samson indicated to his colleagues to crouch low. He quietly pushed his machete into the soft earth, the hilt angled toward him so he could snatch it up at a moment's notice. Then he drew his revolver from his waistband. It would take one shot through the female's skull to kill her, but that was a desperate move. The head was worth more intact. He hoped two shots to the heart would suffice. If he missed, there was a chance she would charge—then it would have to be a headshot.

Samson felt the thrill of adrenalin he always experienced during a hunt, no matter how one-sided it was. In fact, he only ever hunted when the risk of danger was minimal. He quickly checked if his companions had followed his lead.

Jean-Paul had vanished.

During the two-day hike he had been constantly complaining about the weight of the net so it was unlikely, now they had reached their goal, that he would just turn tail and run from the beasts.

Nicolas looked equally baffled by his friend's disappearance, which he silently communicated through a series of frowns and shrugs.

Then a bark echoed across the jungle. Samson was certain they had made no noise, but the band had seen them and were scattering for cover. The female glared at him, incisors bared as she grunted a warning. He was more than aware of the rippling power beneath the fur. He'd heard tales of poachers mauled to death, limbs torn from sockets.

Samson fired a shot. His hand was shaking uncontrollably and the bore of the gun made the shot fall very wide, splintering a trunk ten feet away. The loud report galvanized the female and she pelted into the undergrowth.

Samson knew there was no point in being subtle now; his paycheck was getting away.

"Jean-Paul, move your stinking butt!" he yelled, his accent tinged French. He turned to Nicolas and what he saw chilled him to the core—

His companion seemed to have been hoisted vertically into the boughs of the tree. Samson witnessed Nicolas's shotgun still falling from the man's grasp as the legs silently disappeared into the branches. It happened so fast that Samson briefly thought it was an optical illusion, if it were not for the discarded weapon on the ground. Nicolas must have leapt into the tree for some reason. One thing was for sure—Samson was alone and he had no wish to pursue the startled gorillas without backup.

"Nicolas?" he hissed. "Jean-Paul?"

Only the fleeing gorillas' grunts answered him. Swearing, Samson retrieved his machete and jogged back down the incline to where he had last seen Jean-Paul.

"You pair of idiots! They're runnin' away!" Were his companions hiding from him? Playing some kind of practical joke? "It'll take another day before we find 'em again! Is that what you fools want?"

He reached the fallen shotgun and glanced up. Nicolas's legs dangled in the canopy twenty feet above.

"What ya doin' . . ." his voice trailed off. It was clear Nicolas hadn't ascended the tree by choice. Branches obscured his torso. He wasn't moving; his hands hung limp by his side.

Fear gripped Samson. Had his friend triggered another poacher's trap? Competition for rare game was fierce, often ending in bloodshed.

He moved for a better view. Now he could see the vines around the man's throat. His face was swollen, his eyes lifeless.

"Jean-Paul . . . where are you?" shouted Samson, his voice quivering with fear. He knew in his gut that a similar fate had struck his other companion. Anger suddenly flushed the fear away. A profitable trip had unraveled and left him standing alone in the middle of the deadly jungle.

Sudden movement in the canopy above shifted the anger back into icy fear. The killer was still there.

Something big hurtled through the treetops at great speed. Samson fought rising panic. If it had been another poacher he would have shot Samson already. His superstitious imagination ran wild and he wondered if the gorillas had come back lured by the scent of blood.

Then a howl echoed through the trees. It was inhuman, savage, like nothing he had ever heard before.

Dropping his machete he grabbed the shotgun and blindly fired two shots into the branches. He was sure he hadn't hit anything, but the din stopped.

Nothing stirred.

The hairs on the back of Samson's neck rose in a primeval response to danger. He sensed eyes watching him. He weighed up his options: He could run, but Nicolas and Jean-Paul had carried all the equipment while he had scouted ahead. Without food, water, and a map he wouldn't be able to find his way back to the encampment. He needed to strip the gear from their bodies before he could flee and he still hadn't found Jean-Paul's body.

Samson's keen eyes spotted movement. A large humanoid shape, light brown and hairless, leapt an impossibly wide space between the treetops in a single bound. Samson was too slow to aim, but he fired anyway in a hope the noise would scare his opponent away.

The lofty canopy cast a deep shade, preventing anything else besides waist-high fern thickets to grow below. Samson realized how exposed he was so he raced for cover within the ferns. He made it several yards before his foot snagged a looping root and he fell sprawling to the earth. His gun skittered into the undergrowth and he cursed the fact that he'd left his machete behind.

Blood trickled from Samson's hands, cut on sharp thorns. He tried to ignore the pain, but it had stirred a memory. The figure he had seen swinging above his head reminded him of tales of the White Ape that was said to roam the mountains. Some Elders claimed it was the spirit of a slain silverback gorilla that murdered hunters. Samson had never believed that.

Until now.

Fighting the urge to vomit, Samson crawled through the foliage, flicking away a long black millipede that was crawling across his hand. He scrambled quickly, determined to put distance between him and his assailant. Then he became aware that both hands were damp and sticky. Had he torn them on further thorns? A quick check revealed it wasn't his blood but he had crawled through a stream of it.

His gaze was inexorably drawn to the source: A pockmarked human face peered out of a bush with dead eyes.

Samson's bowels churned and he couldn't stop the whimper escaping his lips. He rapidly scuttled in the opposite direction—ignoring the soft thud of feet landing behind him. It could only be his attacker. Terror propelled Samson onward. He didn't dare look behind. If he could only reach some denser cover than the thickets . . .

Something flicked past his ear with a sharp whoosh. A rough vine noose neatly gripped his neck and a violent jerk forced him onto his back. His blood-slicked fingers groped at the noose as he was dragged backward through the shrubs.

From his prone position, Samson had a fleeting glimpse of the murderer—it was a man. Naked save a ragged pair of cargo shorts, he possessed a deeply tanned body that was as muscular as a Greek god's. The killer had a dark mane of tangled hair, and intense gray eyes peered at him with contempt. Samson tried to pull himself free, but the killer moved with a grace and speed that he couldn't match. A blood-soaked hand drew a tarnished knife and swung it down with precision.

Samson died with a single blow.

Silence fell but for a moment. Then the vicious roar resounded across the mountain. A victory bellow radiating power and dominance of all living things.

It was the roar of Tarzan—Lord of the Jungle.

2

The heavy throb of the chainsaw changed pitch as it was thrust into a branch thicker than a man's arm. Chrome-plated steel teeth effortlessly chewed through the wood. Robbie Canler grinned as he slashed the chainsaw through another limb, pruning the fallen log into a smooth finish. The blade spat splinters of wood at him, which clattered against his eye protectors and covered his sweaty brow in fine sawdust. Hacking things apart with a chainsaw was exactly the kind of fun a teenager should be having, or so he thought.

A firm hand on his shoulder made him jump and he swung the saw around almost cutting Clark in two.

"WHOA!" yelled Clark. "Turn that damn thing off! Didn't you hear me shout?"

Robbie switched the saw off and placed it safely on the ground. He removed his eye protectors and dabbed what little sweat the sawdust wasn't clinging to.

"Sorry. Didn't hear a thing," Robbie answered sheepishly.

Clark must have been in his forties, but Robbie had never dared ask. Half Dutch, half South African, Clark spoke with a pronounced Afrikaans accent. Robbie didn't know too much about his past, other than that he appeared to be a drifter with an uncanny knack of getting involved with illegal activities. He was the one who had found Robbie stowed away on an American freighter destined for Africa when he ran away from home. Clark hadn't asked too many questions, which suited Robbie fine. He hadn't discussed his past with anybody, although he occasionally longed to unburden his conscience.

Until Clark had found him, Robbie had no idea what he should do or where he should go. Fate had led him to the logging expedition where he had found friendship and a surrogate family life. He'd even found Jane, warming to her like the sister he had lost. The situation was perfect because nobody at the camp tended to ask too many questions since the whole operation was illegal.

Clark had taken Robbie under his wing and allowed him to join the loggers as long as he agreed to keep studying. Clark had insisted that it was one thing to run away, but only an education would give the boy somewhere to run to. Robbie had agreed, happy to take advice from the closest he'd ever had to a father figure.

Clark picked up the chainsaw. "You should be in class." *Class* sounded more like *cliss* under his thick accent.

Robbie indicated the tree he was clipping. "I thought it'd be more worthwhile doing this. We're behind on the quota . . ."

"You let Archie and me worry 'bout that. You and I had a deal, remember?"

Robbie weighed up his possible responses, but complaining about the lessons would be futile so he reluctantly trudged back to the huts.

• • •

Jane Porter removed a layer of dust from her iPhone's scratched screen. She was annoyed to see the battery level was bottoming out, the result of a partial recharge when the generator shut off early the previous night.

With a reluctant sigh, she turned her attention back to the yellowing book on the desk in front of her. She was in class . . . well, what passed for a classroom out here. It was nothing more than three wooden walls supporting a corrugated-iron roof that was more rust than metal. It didn't so much keep the frequent rain off than deflect it inward. The last week had been a long dry spell that turned everything to dust but now black clouds hung low on the horizon, threatening to turn the weather again.

The classroom looked out across the dusty camp filled with machinery, gasoline-spewing generators and huts made from anything that could form a wall. They moved the camp every two months to follow the logging operation. It sported a bar, which was the only place for the twenty-two occupants to eat and drink and was where the loggers regularly got drunk. The workers called the camp *Karibu Mji*, Swahili for "Welcome Town," but it was far from welcoming. It certainly wasn't Baltimore. Jane called it hell.

Jane's attention waivered over the dog-eared copy of *The Tempest*, which must have passed through a hundred other grubby hands before reaching hers. The yellowed pages had long gone from possessing a musty book smell, to something biological and rank.

"Jane?" She could just hear the voice above the pounding rock music of track twelve. "Jane?"

With a truculent sigh, Jane pulled the ear buds out and arched a questioning eyebrow at her teacher, Esmée, a huge black woman who appeared to possess an expansive knowledge of everything. But Jane thought the woman's talents were wasted out here trying to teach her.

"You not listenin' to me again."

With a sigh, Jane pulled her iPhone from the pocket of her faded blue jeans and stopped the music. Robbie slouched into the classroom, occupying the only other desk. He was still grimy—there was little point in cleaning up too often out in the jungle.

"Ah, glad you joinin' us, Mister Canler," said Esmée with a smile.

"Wouldn't miss your lesson for the world, Esmée," said Robbie with a cheeky smile.

Jane acknowledged his arrival with a tiny nod, then stared blankly at the words on the page before her. "This is a waste of my time, Esmée. It's not like we have proper tests to pass. None of this is of any real use."

She heard Esmée sigh and a creak of wood indicated her teacher was leaning forward on her desk, looking over the top of her thick lenses, no doubt donated from some far-off charity bin back in civilization.

"An education's a darlin' thing to have. Knowledge don't need tests to be useful. Your papa knows that." Esmée's comment was delivered to the top of Jane's head. "Else why we all here? Or am I wastin' *my* time?"

"I can most definitely say: You are wasting your time." Jane regretted the words the instant they tumbled from her lips. She was in an irritable mood, the humidity was too much to bear and she felt she was nearing her breaking point for staying in the jungle.

Esmée nodded. She never lost her temper. Never argued back. That made Jane feel all the guiltier. She put her head in her hands, resisting the urge to start shouting. She glanced at Robbie, who was watching her curiously. Was that a look of concern or pity?

"I hate it here, Esmée. There's nothing for me! This place is a dump and what friends do I have here? They're all back home."

"You have Robert here."

Jane scowled at Robbie. They were the same age, but that was their only similarity. He was secretive, but they had got on well until he had butted into an argument between her and her father. That was a cardinal sin in Jane's book, but then he had made it worse by accusing her of not appreciating that she had a father who loved her. What did he know? What kind of loving father drags their daughter to a remote African jungle? Since then she had stayed away from Robbie and neither had taken the opportunity to apologize.

Esmée pulled up a wooden stool and sat opposite Jane. Sliding her glasses onto her head she gently took both Jane's hands in her huge hands, and looked her squarely in the eye.

"You ain't lookin' properly. Out there is a land of beauty."

Jane glanced outside again. Black dust, litter, hastily constructed drainage ditches filled with dirty water and a pair of fat cats bathing in the afternoon sun.

"It's a crap shack, Esmée."

Robbie nodded. "She has a point. It's hardly a luxury hotel."

Jane managed a smile, thankful for the support.

Esmée gave them both a measured look.

"You gotta look beyond that. The land out there is more wonderful than anythin' you imagine." Esmée had tried to educate them about the vast range of wildlife around them.

"You mean the land my dad's chopping down?"

A pained look crossed Esmée's face. She was born in Zaire, a country that no longer existed by that name. Now it was known as the Democratic Republic of the Congo. The scars on Esmée's arms and right cheek were testament to the bloody wars and genocide that had ravaged the country. She had survived that only to become a teacher for a bunch of illegal loggers who were now tearing apart her country in a different way. Jane had built a picture of Esmée's life over the last four months only through clues and occasional history lessons. She had no idea how her mentor felt about her father's actions.

Esmée gripped Jane's hands a little tighter. "Mr. Porter, your papa . . ." she faltered, searching for the right words. "He doin' what he's doin' cuz he has ta, not cuz he wants ta."

Jane smiled and slipped her hands away. "That's the kind of trash he's been telling me ever since we got here. It doesn't make sense when he says it either."

Jane was frustrated. She wanted to shout, but knew it was unfair to burden Esmée with her troubles and she no longer trusted Robbie. Out here, she had nobody to confide to; nobody to laugh with. Nobody.

Jane stood up, snatching the iPhone from the table. She stormed from the classroom. Esmée got up so sharply the stool topped over.

"Miss Porter! Where you think you're goin'? Come right back here until I say you can go!"

Jane drowned Esmée out with the music's angst-ridden wailing. She didn't look back; Esmée never followed her and always behaved the next day as though nothing had happened.

Robbie leaned over and took the book Jane had left.

"Shakespeare? OK, I'm willing to give it a shot."

Esmée watched Jane disappear amongst the shacks before she turned her attention to her remaining pupil.

• • •

Jane ignored the workmen returning from the front line. They were a mix of nationalities—Congolese, a few Rwandans, some Zimbabweans who had fled here for a better life, and a couple of Indians. They knew well enough to leave Jane alone, even if her lithe figure and cascading blonde hair made her stand out wherever she went. She headed to the outskirts of Karibu Mji, away from the stench of the communal toilets, stale beer, and sweat.

It was the only form of escape she had.

At the edge of the camp she screamed as loud as she could, knowing the rattle of the generators would drown it out. She cursed her life, her father and mother, and the annoying Robbie Canler who had butted into her business.

Jane vented her anger until tears rolled down her cheeks. Then she collapsed on a tree stump with her head in her hands.

After she had calmed down, she pulled her phone out and her fingers danced across the phone's keyboard as she composed an email to the friends she had been forced to abandon in Baltimore. Her emails were all the same, filled with sorrow and expletives describing the hostile sweat box where she had been dumped. Everything in the jungle—trees, insects, and animals—seemed deadly. It was here she had seen her first dead bodies, loggers who were killed in accidents. It was a place where life seemed cheap.

She hit send and the message filed itself in her outbox, next to the other 142 pleas for help she had written since arriving in the jungle. None of them had been sent. A phone signal was unknown out here.

The jungle was isolation. A wall-less prison.

Jane resisted hurling the phone away. It was the final link she had to her past life and the only thing that was keeping her sane. She stared at the jungle that began yards away from the camp's buildings. Around the perimeter towering trees had been stripped of their lower branches by the workers, as the leaves made the best available substitute for toilet paper. The trunks had since turned gray and lifeless. Darkness lay beyond.

Goosebumps suddenly prickled her arm. She tried to rub them away but couldn't shake the feeling that she was being watched. She found herself drawn to the gloomy trees and could almost sense the malice emanating from them.

• • •

After a very short lesson, Robbie ambled back to the logging operation in time to watch Clark sink his chainsaw into the heartwood of a broad trunk. Clark stopped the moment he felt, and heard, a mighty crack ripple through the mahogany tree. He quickly withdrew the saw and backed away.

"She's going!" he bellowed.

Two other loggers hastily moved away. Clark's incision was perfect and there was little doubt in what direction the tree would fall, but it was better to be safe than sorry.

The trunk of the tree was almost wider than he was. With a wrenching crunch the 120-foot giant keeled over, smashing its way through other trees and crushing the foliage beneath. Robbie felt the ground tremble as ancient roots were ripped to the surface.

Clark whooped victoriously and clapped Archie Porter on the back. Both men were sweating, their shirts black from exertion.

"A few more bucks in the bank, eh?" said Clark.

Archie Porter grinned, more out of habit than humor. "Deserves a beer or three, but we've still got to get her out of here. Light's fading. Trim her off tomorrow, Phil." Archie occasionally teased him with "Phil" from his surname, Philander—a name that got him into many bar fights.

"Light's good for another half-hour, mate," grinned Clark, then he noticed that Robbie had joined them. "What happened to our deal?"

Robbie shrugged. "Esmée didn't feel like it." He glanced knowingly at Archie. "Jane was being a pain again and stormed off." He saw Archie tense at the mention of his daughter.

"Is that a fact? Well, come an' help with this big sucker. We'll get her ready for floatin' tomorrow."

Clark headed toward the tree, yelling orders to the other two loggers in Swahili.

"Rob, hold up a moment," said Archie as he wiped the sweat from his brow with the hem of his shirt. He unclipped the drinking canteen from his belt and took a long hard drink. He still wasn't used to the chlorine taste of the water. Nor was he really used to his new lifestyle. "You said something about Jane?"

Robbie knew this line of questioning would just land him in trouble with Jane.

"She was . . . y'know, same as usual," he replied diplomatically.

Archie's face creased with concern, and Robbie felt a pang of jealousy—*it must be nice to have somebody worry about you. A father who cares for you and would never hurt you.* The kind of family he'd never had . . .

The buzz of Clark's chainsaw shattered the tranquility as he climbed onto the fallen tree and trimmed away the branches. Only one man was helping him, the other was staring up in the trees surrounding the clearing. Not wanting to pursue their conversation any further, Archie and Robbie followed the man's gaze but could see nothing of interest in the thick canopy around them. They slowly approached the man, who went by the name of Mister David. He was a local who Archie trusted enough to be the foreman. His focus on the canopy was intense, suspicious. Archie knew enough to trust local knowledge. Eastern Congo was a dangerous place to be. Drawing level with Mister David, Archie still could see nothing.

"What is it?" he whispered. "Another leopard?"

A leopard had hounded the loggers a few weeks ago. One of the workers had even been attacked so badly he'd lost an arm. Despite Archie's pleas not to kill the creature, he still remembered the day it had been carried into the camp with a bullet hole in the head. He also recalled the horrified expression on his daughter's face. She hadn't spoken to him for a week after that.

"No leopard," whispered Mister David. No other explanation was forthcoming, but the apprehensive look on his face worried Archie.

"What is it then?" asked Robbie as he joined them.

"Not sure. Feels like . . . like we're being watched."

The moment he said the words, Robbie felt his hackles rise. He couldn't see movement, but the sudden fear of being watched . . . of being stalked . . . overcame him.

There was something . . . or *somebody* there. Archie felt it too. A primal instinct warned of nearby danger.

Seconds passed; perhaps even a minute. Then a terrified wail echoed through the clearing. It took a second for Robbie to realize it was coming from behind. He whirled around to see Clark throw his chainsaw aside and leap off the tree. The other man was lying on the ground; even from this distance, Robbie could see he was covered in blood.

"Help me!" roared Clark.

Robbie sprinted over the uneven ground then suddenly halted at the grisly sight. The worker's shirt was ripped in a diagonal slash from left shoulder to his stomach and blood pumped from the wound. Clark's hands were already slick as he tried to apply pressure to keep the wound together. The man shook violently, shrieking with agony, and Robbie felt his stomach churn.

Archie and Mister David ran past him.

"How . . . ?" spluttered Archie as he knelt down.

"The chain snapped an' walloped him."

Robbie shuddered—*that could have been me!*

"Keep the pressure on; keep that wound closed. It's not deep. I don't think any arteries are severed." Archie barked at Mister David: "Get me rope and leaves. The biggest leaves you can find."

Archie moved fast. It had been a while since he'd practiced any of his medical skills. That had been another life; but the knowledge flooded back nevertheless.

So busy were the men saving a life, they didn't notice the subtle movement in the canopy high above. Robbie caught it though, just on the edge of his peripheral vision. It was too fleeting for him to believe it was anything more than his imagination.

He was wrong. They had been watched from the moment they had left Karibu Mji.

They had been watched . . . and they had been judged.

3

"Almost a day drivin' through that?" Clark growled, stabbing a finger toward the dirt trail that was rapidly disappearing into darkness as the sun set behind brooding charcoal clouds. "He'll be dead from fever before we hit the town!"

Archie and Clark had been locked in a fierce argument since they arrived back at Karibu Mji with the injured man. Archie had done all he could to dress the wound with a few vines and leaves, and a little more with the camp's medical kit, but it was far from enough. Robbie tried to force water between the man's lips and mumbled assurances to distract him from the argument. It reminded him too much of the violent arguments back home. Arguments that had led to bloodshed.

"It's worth the chance," snapped Archie. "We're talking about a man's life!"

"Then what, eh? Another day with some charity doc before an air ambulance reaches him. Then we're talking about answerin' some tricky questions, aren't we, mate?"

Archie glowered as he watched Mister David tend to their patient, who had now passed out through blood loss. The silence only lasted a minute before Archie and Clark started again. Robbie knew that if their logging operation was discovered it would land them all a life sentence in some squalid, cramped Third-World cell. That's if they were lucky. He had heard reports of overzealous government teams who had shot first and asked questions later in a bid to stem illegal activities. And if they did manage to avoid the authorities they would still have to avoid the wrath of the guerrillas lurking in the jungle. The rebel soldiers of the FDLR were located close by and seldom hesitated in taking hostages or killing foreigners. One night, while tipsy, Clark had confided in Robbie that he and Archie had made a pact with the rebel leader, Tafari, offering kickbacks that allowed them to pillage the jungle while the rebels didn't interfere and kept any competition away. Robbie was in no doubt that the FDLR would come down on them hard if they did anything to threaten the guerrillas' security.

Mister David interrupted their bickering with a blunt message: The worker had died.

Nobody spoke. Robbie couldn't think of anything to say. He noticed Archie refused to meet Clark's eyes, and occupied himself by organizing a team of men to dig a grave away from Karibu Mji. Robbie had volunteered, but Clark had firmly told him to stand aside. Robbie was thankful; he had no real desire to perform the unpleasant task.

Archie said a few words as the man was lowered into the dirt. He didn't know much about the deceased; he even had to ask around for his name. The pseudonym "Frank" was offered by the closest person the dead man had to a friend. Most of the workers kept away as they thought attending funerals was a bad omen, so Archie filled in the grave alone. He stabbed the shovel repeatedly into the mound of earth with such fury that blisters formed on his hands as if the pain was his penance for not doing more to help the man.

By the time he'd finished the heavens had opened, turning the ground into mud and overflowing the camp's rudimentary drainage system. Water flowed between the huts, washing away any junk that wasn't tied down.

Archie walked to the bar to find Jane standing outside, soaking wet despite sheltering under the porch.

"What're you doing out in this?" he asked.

"I saw what you did, Archie," was Jane's simple answer. She

always called him Archie when she was annoyed, which was often.

Archie slicked back his wet hair and smiled at his daughter, a smile that didn't reach his eyes. "I did what I had to."

"Really? If you hadn't started logging and dragged us all to the middle of this dump, he wouldn't have died!"

The comment stung Archie, and he had no easy reply.

"Why don't we go home, Dad?" It was almost a plea.

"Sweetheart, we've been through this . . ."

"No. You've been through this in your own head. You never listen to me! What if I got ill out here? Would you just let me die too?"

The sly blow hurt Archie, but he tried to hide it.

Jane was still fuming. "I hate it out here. I want to go back to the States! Don't you see how crazy this all is?"

"Go back to what?"

"We could find Mom," Jane said in a hoarse whisper.

Archie watched the rain. There had been many iterations of this conversation. Sometimes shouting, sometimes whispered, none of them pleasant.

"She doesn't want to be found."

"Maybe—"

"She left us *both*, Jane. All she left behind was pain and debt. You have no idea what I went through when we lost everything. Everything I had built for us. All gone because of her selfishness."

"She left *you*!" spat Jane, tears in her eyes. "And then you forced me to leave everything! My friends, my life, for what? This?"

"*Us*. She left us. And 'this' was an opportunity we needed. A last chance to leave our problems behind and create a new nest egg. To start all over."

"By breaking the law?"

"Better I do it here than at home," Archie replied quietly. It wasn't much of an argument, but it was the only one he had. "We desperately need the cash. You know that. Back home, I can't be a doctor again and I couldn't make a quarter of what I get here unless I started knocking over banks or dealing drugs—but I've got some morals, believe it or not. And I've got a duty to look after you."

He saw Jane's fists bunch as she fought her emotions. Archie had always considered himself a good father, but that was before he was expected to raise a teenage daughter with a will stronger than his own. He was out of his depth. In the past he would have hugged her, but these days that usually triggered a tantrum. Instead he just stood and waited for Jane to respond.

She bit her lip and shivered. Her face was pale, her eyes luminous with tears she couldn't shed.

"You must be cold. Let's go inside," she said quietly.

Archie hid his surprise. For once she was being reasonable. He hoped it was a sign of things to come.

The bar was swelteringly warm and unusually quiet, save for the continuous drumroll of rain on the iron roof. The entire workforce was here, staring thoughtfully into their beers. Robbie played pool with an Indian logger, Anil. The table was so old that patches of felt had torn away leaving black tarry streaks. Mister David sat solemnly in the corner with Serge, a logger who had joined the operation at the same time as him. Clark sat at the bar, already on his third beer. Jane sat next to him, her father on the other side.

"A beer for me and something for Jane," said Archie. Esmée served behind the bar when she wasn't teaching and Jane judiciously avoided her gaze. Esmée popped the cap off a Tusker beer for Archie and gave Jane a bottle of cola, slamming it a little harder than usual on the bar.

Nobody said a word. Deaths in the jungle were frighteningly regular, and every couple of months somebody new would turn up as a replacement, lured by the cash the wood brought in.

Jane caught Robbie glancing over with the look of concern he wore every time she argued with Archie. He smiled, although the death had clearly shaken him. Jane smiled back and felt the sudden need to talk to a friend. A loud belch from Clark interrupted her reverie.

"Why do you do this?" Jane suddenly asked him.

Clark finished the dregs of his beer before answering. "Why do I drink or why am I out here rather than with a family back home?"

"Both."

"Because the beer costs less."

"That's lame."

Clark had been a friend of her father's for many years. He was always traveling and, when Jane was younger, she used to enjoy his visits and stories of far-flung places. He had been responsible for suggesting he and Archie start logging in Africa to make their fortunes.

"Jane . . ." said Archie. He knew what she intended.

"It's OK," said Clark, taking another beer that had been automatically replaced by Esmée. "I'm here because I plan to retire early. Go back to South Africa, buy a ranch . . . meet the right *bokkie* and have a dozen *pikkies*. Your problem, kiddo, is you think you're gonna be out here for ever, right?" Jane shrugged. Clark was the only person alive who could get away with calling her "kiddo." "You're not lookin' at the bigger picture."

"No, I'm looking at a blank canvas."

Clark snorted with laughter, beer tickling the back of his nose. "Jeez, Arch, you really have a sharp one 'ere! Sarcastic wit and sharp tongue—that comes from your mother." Jane was bemused by the remark, but Clark pushed on. "You'll be back home soon enough, the difference being, you'll go back rich because of your dad." Clark extended his bottle and clinked Archie's beer, a simple act that immediately absolved their earlier argument.

"That doesn't matter . . ." began Jane.

"Don't it? Listen, Jane, when you get back home you'll have everythin' you ever wanted: your own apartment, new car—a sporty car. Clothes . . . anythin'—all because you and your dad made a bit of a sacrifice now. Trust me, you'll look back on this experience and laugh. And then you'll laugh at all your mates who are strugglin' to make ends meet 'cause they stayed home and didn't chase fortune and glory."

"Fortune and glory?"

"Mother Nature's given all this bounty for us to use. So why not use it, eh?"

Jane didn't answer Clark and Archie began talking about the numbers of logs they needed to shift and the problems floating the logs down the tributaries feeding the mighty Congo River. Logs got snagged, jamming the flow; some even drifted down uncharted branching rivers and were lost. Men had been crushed and drowned between floating logs, and animal attacks were not unknown against the shepherding loggers. Depending on the current, it was a process that could take weeks before the timber reached the waiting lumber boats prior to being shipped off to China, which was their biggest client. Jane blocked the conversation, and began to nod off in her seat.

"You OK?"

Jane's eyes flicked open. It took her a moment to realize Robbie had just spoken to her.

"Just tired." She couldn't stifle a deep yawn.

"I know how you feel . . ."

Jane cut him off. "I'm all talked out, I just want to sleep." She excused herself and slipped from the bar, mumbling her goodnights.

It was still hammering with rain outside. Hurricane lanterns burned around the perimeter of the camp, attracting hordes of insects but deterring the more fearsome predators. She readied herself to run through the mud to her hut—but a voice called behind her.

"Jane! Wait." It was Robbie. "You looked sad today. A lot on your mind, I bet." He paused, uncomfortable with discussing emotions. "I just wanted to say, if you ever need to talk . . ."

"What's there to talk about?" replied Jane frostily, then mentally kicked herself. This was an opportunity to renew their friendship. She softened. "Guess this is a long way from home for you too, huh?"

Robbie smiled. "Just a little. Still, it's better than what I left behind."

"I don't believe that for a second."

A brief flicker of pain crossed Robbie's face. "Believe it. When I stowed away, I didn't know where I was going. Didn't care. And I ended up here."

"You and me both."

"Best move I ever made. I know it's difficult—"

A loud crash suddenly reverberated through the darkness. It sounded like a tree falling, but was followed by a deep bass sound and massive cracking branches, as if something huge was moving through the jungle.

"What is it?" she whispered.

Robbie shook his head. They were both so on edge that they jumped when Mister David spoke from behind them.

"Something has been angered," he muttered.

Jane wasn't comforted by the reply. "Like a lion?" The lions rarely came this high into the rainforest. Mister David shook his head. "An elephant?" Jane didn't believe something as huge as an elephant could move through the dense jungle, but she had been assured forest elephants were out there. She hadn't seen any interesting animals since she had arrived. In fact she had seen more at the Maryland Zoo back in Baltimore.

"Something bigger," muttered Mister David.

Jane shivered. As far as she knew there was nothing bigger than an elephant. The unsettling commotion continued, drawing Archie, Clark, and a few others out.

"What the hell is that?" said Clark. "Sounds like a bulldozer."

A quick check across the camp revealed the team's rusting bulldozer was still there, thick metal chains coiled behind it, tough enough to drag the felled trees away.

A terrifying howl suddenly echoed through the night. An unearthly blend of savage animal and tormented spirit.

"*Negoogunogumbar*," muttered one of the Congolese workers, crossing himself.

"What's a *Negoogunogumbar*?" asked Robbie. He had a gift for languages so his tongue picked up the word easily enough.

Mister David replied in a low whisper that made his words all the more ominous. "The spirit of the jungle: a giant that eats children and brings ill fortune. Some say he comes in the night as a demon. Sometimes a white ape; sometimes an invisible spirit that slits men's throats."

"That's just superstition," cautioned Archie. "Maybe . . . maybe it's a troop of gorillas. There are some, out toward the mountains."

"If gorillas can make that kinda racket," hissed Robbie, "then I'd hate to get on the wrong side of them."

• • •

The rain abated the following morning, but the mystery intensified. During the night the bulldozer's engine cover had been wrenched open by some Herculean force. Wires and coolant tubes had been slashed and yanked from the engine block along with the fuel injectors. However, there were no footprints in the mud around the vehicle. No sign of the saboteur.

Negoogunogumbar was again whispered amongst the loggers. Archie had tried to quash the rumor by laying suspicion on Tafari, the rebel general, and the first person Archie had suspected since the rebels had started demanding a larger cut of the profits.

Clark examined the damage. "Think you can fix her?" he asked Robbie.

Robbie was pleased to be asked. Back in the States he had worked in a garage from an early age and considered himself an adept mechanic. He had repaired the camp's jeep several times. Robbie inspected the damage with a keen eye.

"I suppose. We should have the parts in the supply shack, but it will take the better part of the day."

Archie cursed under his breath. "We're not going to float that mahogany in the river tonight. Why would Tafari do something like this?"

Clark shook his head. "Can't be him, mate. This only delays them getting paid and they need the money to buy arms. Poachers, maybe?"

That left the unanswered question as to why poachers would do such a thing. Robbie busied himself with fixing the bulldozer. He was glad to have something to take his mind away from the unsettled atmosphere around him. Archie and Clark spent forty minutes calming the loggers. It was difficult to get the superstitious men back into the jungle to search for valuable hardwoods, but Archie couldn't afford to have them standing idly around since they were behind their quotas.

However, more strange news came back from the jungle. Mister David was out of breath when he returned at a run.

"It's gone! The tree . . . it has gone!"

A creeping paranoia settled over the camp as Archie and Clark followed Mister David. Jane insisted on accompanying them; she was feeling too nervous to be left behind.

They reached the clearing where their mahogany trophy had lain the day before. It wasn't there any more.

"How the hell did that happen?" yelled Clark in astonishment. He held up a finger to stop Mister David before he could utter the evil spirit's name.

"There must be other loggers in the area," said Archie. If that were true it made their situation even more dangerous. The fight for dominance could get bloody.

Mister David picked out a trail that led from the clearing. The earth was furrowed from where the tree had been dragged out. It led a hundred yards before ending in a steep precipice that was hidden by foliage. It dropped a hundred feet to boulders and dense vegetation below. Poking through the bushes were the roots of the mahogany.

"Why just toss it off the cliff?" asked Jane.

"It's not the why that bothers me. It's the how," said Clark darkly. "No machinery cut through here so it wasn't dragged off the cliff, it was pushed."

"Unless it walked itself," said Mister David.

Clark snorted. "Are you sayin' your jungle spirit is also a walkin' tree? You can cut that out now."

"That's what it sounded like last night," said Jane.

Clark shot her a stern look; she wasn't helping.

"Not a word to the others," warned Archie. "Keep this between us. I don't need them getting wound up." He looked at Mister David. "An extra fifty dollars for your mouth to stay shut."

Jane wandered away from the conversation that swiftly turned into haggling as Mister David seized the opportunity to raise his fee. A dash of color amongst the verdant greens stood out. Jane carefully walked through the undergrowth until she reached a red flower. It was a delicate orchid, vibrant petals curved in exquisite shapes.

Jane went to pluck it; it would cheer up her drab bedroom. Her arm brushed the broad leaves of a fern and, as her fingers closed around the stem, she suddenly noticed something big and ugly had crawled onto her wrist.

For a moment she was paralyzed with fear.

It was a green insect the size of her palm, sporting a nasty pair of forearms and mandibles that Jane was convinced could pluck her eyeballs out. As it slowly crawled up her arm, Jane could feel every leg through her shirtsleeve. Then she finally found her voice and screamed.

"Jane!" Archie bolted over, a revolver clutched in one hand. It took him a moment to register the danger was on her arm, which she held rigid. He laughed with relief as he brushed the bug to the ground. "I told you not to wander off in the jungle."

Jane scratched her arm to get rid of the tingling sensation that lingered from where the insect had crawled. "I didn't! You were just over there!"

"It's easy to get lost out here," Archie warned her. "Just a couple of yards away from the trail and you can get disorientated. It can be impossible to find your way back."

"I know that!" snapped Jane. "Why do you always overreact?"

Jane joined Mister David back at the ravine edge. Archie looked between his daughter and the harmless praying mantis crawling away under some dead leaves. Why does *he* overreact?

• • •

Despite his generous bribe to keep silent, Mister David's mood did not improve. The walk back to Karibu Mji was frequently interrupted because he thought he'd caught movement in the trees. His uneasiness rubbed off on Jane, who was still jittery from her close encounter with the insect. At one point she thought she saw something out of the corner of her eye—a figure partially obscured by broad leaves. But by the time she'd turned her head it had disappeared.

Back at Karibu Mji, Archie and Clark announced they were going to make contact with the FDLR to see if they could shed any light on the inexplicable events. Jane was forced into class with Esmée, who treated her to a warm smile, yesterday's tantrum forgotten.

Jane sat through math in relative silence. The lesson provided a welcome distraction from the thoughts of what was lurking out in the jungle. She loathed the wilderness around her more than ever, and was longing for the security of concrete and glass.

Mister David hung around the shacks, a shotgun slung over his shoulder. Jane suspected her father had ordered him to keep an eye on her. She occasionally saw Robbie crossing to the supply shack, his hands and face smudged with oil. Despite his deal with Clark, he was always avoiding lessons by insisting practical tasks were a priority. She was beginning to envy him.

The rest of the day passed without drama. Workers returned from their recess in the jungle, reporting what precious trees they had discovered, including several rare rosewood. Night came but there was no sign of her father returning from his meeting with the rebels. This was yet another worry Jane could do without.

Esmée assured her everything was perfectly fine. Because they had departed late, Archie and Clark wouldn't have reached the FDLR camp before dark. The jeep they took would only get them a part of the way there; the rest would have to be made on foot through the valley. They had done the route before, so had taken tents and provisions to see them through the night.

In the bar's kitchen, Jane ate a stew Esmée had prepared for the loggers. She looked up when Robbie sat with her.

"You know, in a couple of days me and Clark will be heading into town for fresh supplies. Want to come with us?"

Jane looked at him in surprise. The nearest supply town was almost a day away by jeep. It had been over a month since she had last been anywhere that resembled civilization.

"Sure," she beamed.

"They've got an Internet connection there now. I was wondering what was happening in the rest of the world."

"I thought you liked it out here?"

"I don't know about *like*. I just said it was better than a lot of other places. But to be honest, I know there are a lot of places better than New York."

Jane tried not to smile over the fact she had gleaned a little information about Robbie, who was usually so tight-lipped.

"So that's where you're from."

Robbie realized his slip of the tongue. He shrugged, but didn't comment further. Instead they both listened to the conversations flowing around them as they ate.

Talk in the bar turned to superstitious murmurs, which Jane was sure would spoil her sudden good mood. She retired to her room, lay on her hard bed, and cranked her music to maximum volume.

One of the camp's cats joined her, curling up on her stomach to sleep. Jane idly scratched its head and felt the animal purr. It was a cathartic exercise and she felt her eyes slowly closing as she drifted into a deep slumber.

. . .

It was the feline's sharp claws digging into her stomach that woke Jane. She sat bolt upright, the cat leaping gracefully to the floor, hissing at the door. Jane pulled her headphones out. The music had masked the shouting outside. A pair of gunshots cracked.

She ran to the door, opened it a fraction and saw people running in the darkness. Her first thought was they were being raided by an anti-poaching patrol. She opened the door a little more and the cat made a swift exit. People were running to the supply shack on the edge of the camp, which was ablaze. Orange flames leapt skyward and thick black smoke blotted out the full moon. Buckets of water were thrown over the fire but did little to combat it as more gunshots rang out. Mister David was several feet away from her, shooting into the darkness, Robbie at his side. He glanced at Jane.

"We need help with the fire!" he barked, before running after Mister David.

Jane was confused. Who were they shooting at? As she ran from her hut, toward the fire, she saw Esmée waddling as fast as she could, carrying a cooking pot filled with water. Jane took one of the handles to help her. The intense heat of the blaze made it uncomfortable to get close enough to throw the water but they persevered.

"I'll fill it up!" shouted Jane over the roar of the flames.

She sprinted toward the nearest drainage gully, which was still swollen from the previous night's rainfall. Jane forced the pot into the murky water and heaved it out just as an explosion rocked the supply shack from within. The sides of the shack blasted outward, flinging burning wooden spars and unidentified charred contents. Esmée was so close to the explosion that she was thrown backward.

"Esmée!"

She dropped the pan, intending to help Esmée, but before Jane could take a step, part of a burning roofing plank landed inches in front of her—flipped over and cracked her across the head.

Bright lights flooded her vision and the world around her swam. Jane's legs turned to rubber and she staggered as the cacophony around her grew dim. She stumbled sideways—then something smacked her across the face: a branch. She felt a stab of pain and tripped forward, twisted her ankle, and tumbled flat on her face. There was a blur of movement as the ground escaped from under her and she tasted bitter mud.

For several long moments it felt as if she was underwater—her limbs cycled uselessly until something hard slammed into her chest. The noises around her faded into a void of nothingness.

4

A gentle tickle on the arm woke Jane.

The cat, probably.

She pushed it away, her hand brushing wet fur. The patter of tiny feet and the sound of rustling made her eyes flick open in alarm. She was lying on her side, feet submerged in the river, thankfully not face down or she would have drowned.

The previous night's events flooded back. She tried to sit up, but pain racked her body, she gasped in panic.

OK, calm down, she mentally cajoled. *Arms* . . . she moved her left arm, the one nearest to her face. Her fingers wriggled. *Good, now* . . . she couldn't see her other hand but could feel damp wood under her fingertips. *So far, so good.*

She flexed both feet and was pretty sure she could feel them. *No spinal injuries then*, at least, that's what she thought that meant.

Moving slowly, Jane rolled over. Her back ached as she sat upright and examined herself: clothing stained with mud and one bare foot where she'd lost a sneaker. Moving her limbs hurt because of multiple bruises and her head still swayed. Looking around, her heart skipped a beat—she could see nothing but jungle. She recalled her father's dire warning about wandering off and felt her panic return.

Think, dammit. Something hit me on the head . . .

Her hand automatically touched her forehead where the roof beam had struck her. It stung; dried blood revealed a deep cut the size of her thumb at the base of her hairline and her hair was matted with mud and dried blood. The one thing she had paid attention to was her father's safety briefing when they had arrived in the Congo. He'd shown her dozens of pictures of poisonous reptiles, insects, and plants: nature's most deadly list. He'd also stressed the importance of tending to any wound, no matter how small. Out here infection was the number one killer. She considered bathing the wound in the water, but one glance at the swollen river, brown from mud's natural tannic acids, changed her mind.

I tripped . . . slid down a gully . . .

Thick forest surrounded her. There was no incline she could have descended.

Lost!

The word frosted her heart. She involuntarily shivered as a chill spread through her body despite the humid atmosphere.

Her hand suddenly shot to her pocket. Her phone! She slid it out and was dismayed to see the screen was cracked and wet. Her finger moved to the power button . . . then she hesitated. Back in Baltimore, she had dropped her phone in a puddle and thought it was ruined. The clerk at the store had told her not to switch it back on as it would short circuit. Instead, she took it home and let it dry out over several days. When she had turned it on, it worked as good as new. The problem was, she didn't have a couple of days to wait. But then again, she didn't have a signal either.

"Hello?" the words came out as a croak, her mouth parched. She stood, every muscle aching. It was then she realized she'd been lying in the fork of a broken tree limb that had washed up on the side of the bank with her. The branch had saved her life by keeping her afloat as she was borne away from Karibu Mji.

How far?

"Anyone? I'm lost!" A tickle in her throat reduced her words to a dry hacking cough. She needed to find drinkable water.

Think . . . calm down. If I head upstream, the camp's got to be that way. I can't have drifted far and they'll be looking for me.

It was a plan, it was something to cling to. It allowed her to ignore the dark thoughts that threatened to crowd her mind: *If they were looking for me, why haven't they found me already? Surely Robbie would have noticed?*

Jane followed the riverbank for several feet before she became aware of movement in the trees. A monkey sat on a branch, watching with black eyes beneath its shaggy brow.

"Do you know which way the camp is?" rasped Jane, desperate for any form of interaction. The monkey scratched its backside then examined its fingers, taking great delight in eating whatever it had found. Then Jane remembered she had pushed something furry aside when she woke. "Was that you?"

The monkey looked at her quizzically, then shuffled along the branch. Jane thought it would disappear into the dense boughs; instead it angled an upturned broad leaf and water flowed into its mouth. Jane was struck by how human the motion was.

She saw the same plant clung to the lower parts of the tree, gracing the trunk right down to the ground. She moved closer, examining the cupped leaves that held clear rainwater. Jane greedily drank the contents of one, and then poured another two. The inside of her mouth came alive. The water tasted a little grassy from the chlorophyll, but it was not unpleasant. She looked back at the monkey.

"Thank you!" her voice had returned.

The monkey scratched itself, looking bored. Evidently the entertainment value of talking to a human had been exhausted. With a quick bound the animal disappeared up the trunk.

Jane felt suddenly alone . . . no . . . not alone. Eyes were still on her. She looked around. The feeling of being watched was intense, the same primal instinct that cautioned a grazing animal that danger was near. Wary, Jane continued upriver.

It was impossible to measure time, especially as the sun would often hide behind the lofty canopy. She kept a watchful eye on the banks, keen to identify the gully she had fallen from. Instead all she saw was impenetrable forest.

She lost count of the number of times the river meandered sharply away. Jane couldn't follow it from the bank as her path was blocked by moss-covered rocks and thick gnarled tree roots. She feared that the simple act of walking around the obstacle would take her away from the river and then she would be utterly lost. The river was life, her lifeline back to camp. She waded into the water rather than lose sight of it. Even close to the bank it came to her knees, other times she was waist deep, forced to cling to overhanging branches in case the bank suddenly sheered away.

An occasional splash or suspicious ripple on the water's surface reminded her that crocodiles were common here. Twice she heard a deep snort, but couldn't pinpoint its location. She could only pray it wasn't a hippo. Esmée had told her how, despite their comical appearance, hippos were aggressively territorial.

The hike was made even harder because of the missing shoe. Mud squelched between her toes one moment, a sharp thorny branch would prick her the next. Jane lost count of how many times she had stubbed her toes on hidden rocks.

The second problem was her rumbling stomach. She was surrounded by lush vegetation, some of which was surely edible. But which? For every edible fruit there was something poisonous, something that would send daggers through her stomach and kill her without mercy in minutes.

Pull yourself together, she commanded. In her head, she sounded like her father. The sun was almost overhead. *I couldn't have drifted that far . . .* How many times had she convinced herself of that? Yet the riverbanks never parted to reveal the gully she had fallen down. Hours had passed and she was feeling weak, shaking from hunger. She'd kill for a chocolate bar.

Several times she caught movement in the trees and was convinced the monkey was trailing her, although she never saw it. A variety of caws from unseen birds sounded from all around. With every step they appeared to get louder. She couldn't recall the jungle ever sounding so alive.

Jane trudged out of the water for the dozenth time. The riverbank was now broadening out and felt like muddy sand beneath her naked foot. She looked down, noticing her foot was covered with black gelatinous streaks.

Streaks that pulsed.

Leeches.

Jane gagged, watching their slimy bodies expand as they gorged on her blood. Panicking, she tried plucking them off with a sharp tug. They came free, but the parasites' heads still clung to her flesh with hooked teeth. She twisted the bulbous heads off, tearing skin away.

"Get off me!" Jane screamed. "I hate it out here!" she shouted to the trees above. "I wanna go home! I wanna have coffee, a roof . . . somewhere things don't keep biting me!" She was ranting now, venting aloud what she normally kept to her silent emails.

Jane dropped to her knees and cradled her head. She had been through the emotional wringer when her parents had separated and was now determined not to shed a single tear ever again. She was not sure how long she crouched, but finally decided she had to do something. She stood and blood trickled from her feet, tingeing the sand red. With every ounce of willpower, she forced herself on, hoping, praying, that Karibu Mji lay just beyond the next bend.

Minutes stretched beyond incalculable time as Jane followed the wide bank. Birds no bigger than sparrows, sporting fabulous bright-red plumage, appeared in the trees, chirping melodiously and watching her with interest. Esmée had told her they were bar-breasted firefinches. She had seen a couple around the camp, but never so many. There were dozens in the canopy above her. Although pretty, Jane couldn't shake the feeling they were scrutinizing her like hungry vultures.

As she watched the finches she saw that something was not quite right. At first she couldn't figure it out, until she realized the tree line beyond the birds, visible through a natural break in the canopy, seemed to rise upward. The perspective looked wrong. A nearby group of rocks rose to twice her height and provided an easy climb so she could take in her new surroundings.

She was looking at the slope of a steep mountain that wore the rainforest like a cloak. Clouds hugged every contour and blotted out the peak. Cloud forest: Her father had mentioned it when they first flew into the rainforest. Her stomach lurched. It was a mountain that she had never seen before from Karibu Mji. She must be miles from the camp.

Breaks between the trees showed her the river forking in three different directions, each tributary meandering into the distance. She had reached a convergence of three narrow tributaries that flowed into the one single trunk she had been following. Her heart sank—she could have drifted down any of the three tributaries, but which one? The jungle offered no clues.

She jumped from the rocks and sank to her knees on the riverbank. Jane wanted to cry but emotions still refused to surface. Then she sensed something; a primeval instinct told her that something was stalking her. She was flooded with adrenalin the very moment she heard a noise behind her.

She twisted around, her every move appearing slow and sedate. Her hunter was cautiously striding from trees and issuing a sonorous growl that paralyzed her.

5

The jeep's suspension groaned and creaked alarmingly as it bounced down the narrow trail to Karibu Mji. Archie weaved the vehicle around the frequent potholes and rocks, but still the ride was spine-jarring. Clark gripped the dash with one hand, the door with the other. The open windows were the only form of air-conditioning the vehicle had and both men were sweating heavily.

They were fuming over the meeting with the FDLR leader, Tafari, a hulking man who was pure muscle and malice. He had taken umbrage when asked if the FDLR had sabotaged the logging operation. They were more than familiar with Tafari's quick temper but had caught him in an objectionable mood following the death of his brother during a poaching expedition. He scowled at them, his hateful face wreathed in foul-smelling tobacco from the cigar he rolled between his forefinger and thumb. Half his left ear was missing—some said from a shrapnel wound during the last conflict. Others said it was from when he singlehandedly wrestled a silverback to death.

Archie had tried to be tactful; however, Clark's direct manner had inflamed Tafari so much that he had demanded a ten percent increase on their payments for safe passage through the jungle. Surrounded by thirty armed rebels, including Tafari's lieutenant, a bear of a man named Bapoto, Archie was in no position to haggle. However, he had managed to wangle a promise from Tafari that the rebels would scour the area for any rival loggers.

So it was that both men returned to Karibu Mji in a foul mood; financially worse off and with no clear idea who had disrupted their operation the previous day.

The burned-out supply shack was the first thing that greeted them when they entered the camp. Only Robbie, Esmée, and Mister David were in the village and their faces forewarned of more bad news. Esmée wore a thick bandage taped to the side of her cheek and looked exhausted.

"Es, what happened?" Archie asked before he'd even exited the jeep.

"Just caught a burn. I'll live."

Clark jumped out, his gaze fixed on Robbie. "You OK?"

"I'm fine."

Clark stared at the wreckage of the shack in despair. "That's the last of our supplies gone. Anyone else hurt?"

"Mister Porter, sir—" Esmée began with a stutter.

"Jane has gone," Robbie blurted.

Archie blinked, uncomprehending. "Gone?"

"Jane is *missing*," Esmée clarified. She rushed forward and gripped Archie's hand, her eyes filled with despair. "She was helpin' me douse the fire when somethin' exploded inside. We were all knocked to the ground, that's when I caught this." She tapped her cheek. "When I looked up . . . she'd clean gone."

"I wanted to look for her straightaway," said Robbie. He scowled at Mister David. "But they wouldn't let me!"

Archie looked between Esmée and the wreckage, stunned.

"We searched every building and the surrounding area last night," Mister David chipped in, glaring at Robbie. "No sign of her."

"The jungle . . . ?" Archie's voice came in a whisper.

"We looked as far we could. Since this morning I have the men out searching," assured Mister David.

"They wouldn't let me go with them," complained Robbie.

"Good," snapped Clark. "Can't be doin' with you both lost out there."

Robbie's cheeks burned with anger and embarrassment that even Clark thought he couldn't help search for Jane.

Archie looked Mister David in the eye. "And?" He knew the question was redundant, but it needed asking.

"Nothing yet."

Archie felt weak, and leaned on the jeep's bonnet for support.

"Who did this?" demanded Clark. "Who was responsible?"

"We don't know," replied Esmée. "Don't think it was no accident, though. We saw someone run away." She looked at Mister David for confirmation.

"*Something*," added Mister David in a low voice.

"The saboteurs struck again," snarled Clark. "Just when we weren't here!"

"Could they have taken Jane?" asked Archie, his head in his hands. The Democratic Republic of Congo was not unknown for its human trafficking. People often vanished, put to work in the diamond, copper, or gold mines.

Clark laid a firm hand on his friend's shoulder. "We'll get her back, mate. Even if we have to turn over heaven 'n' hell. We'll get her."

Before Archie could reply a group of excited voices spilled into camp. A party of four workers ran toward them, babbling in Swahili. Archie didn't understand. He didn't need to.

They were holding aloft his daughter's sneaker.

• • •

The guttural snarl resonated through Jane's ribcage. She felt it through the sole of her naked foot. Her eye caught movement in the water—a crocodile? But that wasn't the immediate threat.

The lioness stepped from the dense foliage where she had patiently stalked her prey. She was far from her usual hunting ground, but the scent of Jane's blood had spurred her on. Powerful muscles rippled under the cat's sleek tawny fur. Her eyes never flinched from her quarry; ears pricked as she ignored any other distraction. Her wide paws sank slightly in the sand, lethal black claws extended, recently sharpened on the trunk of an Angouma tree.

Jane didn't dare look away from the predator, and her peripheral vision revealed no close branches or rock she could use for a weapon. The lioness was huge. One swipe of the powerful claws would be enough to eviscerate her. In her panic, Jane raised her hands and snarled back at the beast.

"GRRRAAGH!" her voice sounded weak and pathetic—but the lioness was startled. Jane took a brave step forward and inhaled to roar again, but the beast suddenly charged toward her.

Jane expected a roar, but there was nothing but heavy breathing and the dull thump of paws as they gained traction on the sand. The big cat pounced, jaws extended revealing yellow razor-sharp teeth.

Jane's final image would be the animal's gullet. But she wouldn't go down without a fight. She swung a tiny bunched fist at the lioness in a feeble attempt to save herself.

Then a volley of movement burst out from the left.

A huge shape cannoned into the lioness, knocking the killer aside—but not before a paw slashed Jane's thigh, tearing a strip from her jeans and drawing blood.

Jane fell with a shriek and watched in astonishment as a man tackled the lioness to the ground. Momentum carried both toward the river and they splashed about in a wild frenzy, the water frothing about them.

A claw struck the man on his bare chest—but he didn't seem to notice. He delivered a powerful punch to the beast's ribcage and they both toppled backward with a mighty splash. A terrible roar filled the air and Jane saw that the man had the animal in a chokehold from behind, pulling the beast upright and silencing it. Again they thrashed, water spuming beneath them. More wrestling, then the lioness flipped over and they disappeared beneath the water.

Seconds later the lioness sprinted out of the river, barreling straight for Jane. Jane's heart missed a beat—had her rescuer been killed? She braced herself for the violent attack . . .

But the lioness shot past, blood flowing from a torn ear, ignoring Jane completely as she retreated into the forest.

The adrenalin suddenly vanished, leaving Jane more exhausted than she'd ever felt. The cut on her leg was painful, and she could feel her grip on consciousness slipping.

She watched in a dreamlike state as the man strode from the river. He wasn't too much older than she was. He looked perfect, an Adonis, like the sculptures she'd seen in a museum. Every muscle was defined across his tanned physique. He wore only a pair of ripped shorts that had seen better days. As she started to lose consciousness, she saw that he was bleeding from the gash on his chest and his hands were bloodied too. He bellowed a terrifying warbling cry, a symphony of power and triumph as he beat his chest with one hand. It was the sound of a feral animal, not a man. Darkness clouded Jane's thoughts: Was he her savior or another danger she had to face?

Then she blacked out.

• • •

Jane's next waking moments were a confused strobe of images, sounds, smells, and senses.

She regained consciousness to a gentle swaying motion. Every muscle in her body ached and, judging from her position, she was slumped over her savior's shoulder. Her eyes fluttered open and she saw a sun-beaten back that sported a network of scars. She just had time to register how far away the ground looked, before she lost consciousness again.

A more violent motion awoke her. She blinked several times, not quite comprehending why the ground was racing beneath her—far beneath her. Then it became apparent—she was being carried through the towering trees a hundred feet above the ground. Branches became a blur as the pace increased. Daylight was fading when she got a clear view from the canopy—the far-off treetops looked like broccoli, extending for countless miles and bathed in a crimson sunset.

She closed her eyes and accepted the fevered dream.

• • •

Daylight. She could discern that much through her closed eyelids and the heat on her face. She could hear more birds than she'd ever heard before, their varied calls blending into a natural harmony. There was a background thrum, possibly machinery like the generator back in Karibu Mji, and she could smell something like sweet onions.

She opened her eyes and looked straight into the face of her nurse. They were brown, intelligent eyes . . . but the rest of the face was confusing. A broad flat nose sat above a wide protruding mouth, the leathery skin as black as midnight. Coarse black fur surrounded the face and a massive black hand gently scratched its cheek. The beast was huge, twice as large as Jane.

Jane bit back a scream. The creature was almost nose-to-nose, sniffing her golden hair. She knew what it was: a mountain gorilla. She'd seen them on TV.

The gorilla was satisfied she was awake and backed away, sitting on its haunches as it reached for a large plant frond and delicately began eating it, flexible lips selecting the choicest shoots.

Jane gathered her courage and sat up, taking in her surroundings.

"I've got to be dreaming," she muttered.

She was in a low curved cave with layers of dried grass and branches bunched to make a rudimentary bed. The gorilla was not the only occupant; a small ape, the size of a human toddler, was rolling in the grass. It lay upside down, studying Jane quizzically. The likeness to a human child was incredible. The youngster blew a raspberry with its lips then picked at Jane's remaining shoe, which he had managed to remove.

A large opening ran half the length of the cave and gave a spectacular view across the jungle below. The opening was lined with snaking vines and brightly colored flowers that attracted large, vivid butterflies. Jane crawled to the edge of the cave moving slowly so as not to startle the gorilla. The small ape followed her.

She stepped out of the cave onto a large plateau of rocks. The view took her breath away. Massive tree branches curled around the furthest section of the cave that stood on the edge of a fifty-foot sheer drop to a small lake below.

The lake was formed by a circular caldera. The crystal-clear water glistened in the midday sun, fed by a waterfall that cascaded not far from the cave. Water plumes shimmered in the sun, creating ethereal rainbows.

Further along the plateau the drop gave way to a steep tree-lined trail that snaked down to the lakeshore. Beyond, Jane could see nothing but jungle and occasional clouds that hugged the treetops, giving it a magical appearance. Behind her, the wide platform was surrounded by dense forest that was alive with a myriad of colorful birds. The peak of the mountain towered above, puncturing the blue sky. The only word Jane could think of was "paradise."

Dozens more gorillas sat around the oasis. Females, with youngsters, sat at varying points along the leafy trail and several male blackbacks lolled in the sun, eating whatever they could reach.

Despite her fear, Jane couldn't help but smile . . . a smile that faltered when she realized a huge silverback male was standing at the end of the plateau, staring at her. If she thought the female had been huge, this specimen was massive. He stood on all fours, his front shoulders hunched to his ears. The mouth hung open, displaying lethal canine fangs. Jane looked into the unfriendly eyes that were surrounded by a network of scars from battles long ago.

A bad mistake.

The silverback took the eye contact as a challenge and it coughed twice, posturing to show off his incredible bulk. The small gorilla that had followed Jane outside now ran back into the cave, frightened. The silverback barked and thumped its chest with a loud flat sound that carried over the lake, then it charged forward like a locomotive. Jane was petrified; standing at the edge of the cliff she had nowhere to go. Instead she held her ground and diverted her eyes, waiting for a powerful fist to strike her.

But it didn't come. The silverback barked louder as it stopped inches from her. She could smell the wild garlic on its breath, and her hair ruffled as the ape bellowed. Its fists pounded its chest with a distinctive POK-POK-POK! Then it tore up clods of earth round her, tossing them into the air as it furiously hooted. It was a frightening display of power and Jane's entire body trembled. She suddenly heard chuckling that sounded almost human.

"*Kerchak!*"

The gorilla immediately stopped ranting. It gave Jane one last hoot, before retreating into the undergrowth with a slow arrogance. Jane turned to see who had spoken—and was doubly surprised.

It was her savior. Now he was clean, his wounds bathed. An unruly mop of shoulder-length black hair framed a chiseled face and his gray eyes studied her with interest. A dagger and a coil of vine rope hung from the waistband of his shorts. Every inch of his sculpted physique was muscled.

He crouched on top of the cave, which Jane now realized was no natural refuge—it was an airplane some eighty feet long that had crashed into the plateau, tearing a huge gash in the fuselage, which now functioned as the exit. One wing had been torn off against the mountain, the other extended over the cliff top, forming a perfect diving board into the lake below. Time had covered every inch of the jet with moss and creepers, so, from the air, it was flawlessly camouflaged.

Jane jumped as the stranger threw a dead bush pig at her feet. It had been killed so recently it was still bleeding. Jane automatically crawled away from the carcass.

The man jumped gracefully down with only the faintest rustle of leaves. He took a cautious step toward Jane, crouched on all fours, his eyes appraising her.

Jane brushed her matted hair from her face; her fingers grazed the wound on her forehead. It felt different. A quick check revealed she had been cleaned, and the wounds on her head tended to with a thick sap-like substance that glued the skin together. The slash on her leg had been cleaned and stapled together with unusual small beads. He had saved her from certain death and treated her injuries, so she forced herself to relax. Surely he meant no harm, even if he had just thrown a dead pig at her.

He was tall and broad; Jane only came up to his shoulders. She noticed a network of long-healed scars across his body and a circular patch of skin around his shoulder that had not healed properly. Jane could only imagine a gorilla had taken a chunk long ago.

"You," he said, staring at her intently.

Jane frowned. "Me?" The response only served to confuse the man. Jane groaned inwardly, perhaps he was a little simple.

"*Ninyi?*"

Jane shook her head. "I don't know what you're saying."

He peered at her a little longer. The intensity of his gaze was frightening; the eyes of a killer. However, his expression was neither hostile nor friendly. The gorilla that had nursed Jane in the aircraft appeared in the cave entrance to watch, while her baby capered up and down the fuselage.

"Tana," said the man, pointing to the female gorilla. He indicated to her baby. "Karnath." He stabbed a finger to the trees where the reprimanded silverback sat alone. "Kerchak."

He gently took Jane's trembling hand and pressed it to his chest: "Tarzan." Jane suddenly understood as he pressed her own hand against her chest and said "You?"

"Oh, my name? Why didn't you say?" Tarzan blinked in confusion. "I'm Jane." She indicated to herself. "Jane Porter." Tarzan echoed. "Jane." Then he pointed at the pig. "*Horta*. Eat."

"I couldn't possibly . . ."

Jane watched in disbelief as Tarzan bit into the pig and tore a strip of hairy flesh with his teeth. He happily chewed and nodded to the pig again.

Jane felt a chill of horror, transfixed by Tarzan's bloodstained teeth as he devoured the meat.

Tarzan smiled and once again sank his jaws into the raw flesh.

6

Robbie stared down the mudslide where they had found Jane's sneaker. She had either slipped down there or had been taken against her will. He clambered down, using tree roots to support him. At the bottom, the recent rain had turned the babbling brook into a torrent that could have easily swept an adult downstream. They found no further signs of Jane or their attackers so guessed that they had taken to the water. Archie and Clark were racked with indecision about what to do next, which only served to frustrate Robbie.

He had been indecisive for months, back in New York, and it had led to terrible things. He wasn't about to let history repeat itself.

In his shack, Archie had gathered what supplies he could and stuffed them into a backpack. He'd loaded a shotgun while Clark and Mister David attempted to make him see reason.

"You do not know the jungle," warned Mister David.

"Mate, you go peltin' out there without prep and you'll be in the same sinkhole she is!" said Clark.

"I'm better prepared," snapped Archie. He pointed at Mister David, "And you can come with me."

"Of course," said Mister David, "when we have the equipment to search properly."

Archie turned for the door, but Clark blocked his path. "She's a tough girl. That gives us time to prepare! You ain't as young as you used to be."

From his vantage point at the door, Robbie could see Archie's shoulders sag in defeat. Clark played his trump card.

"If Tafari is behind this, *if* those brutes have taken her . . . at least she'll still be alive. Even they wouldn't risk hurting her, she's worth too much as a ransom."

Archie's knuckles whitened as he gripped his shotgun. "If they're behind this, they're not getting away with it."

Clark put a comforting hand on Archie's shoulder. "You're not wrong, mate. And we're behind you." Robbie could see Clark meant every word, but Mister David didn't look convinced. "But let's be smart, eh? Let's think about this."

Archie leaned the shotgun against the wall and nodded. He crossed to the window and nervously rubbed his stubble.

"We have to tell the authorities. Get an air search in."

"That will mean dismantling the camp," warned Mister David. "If they find us . . ."

Archie shrugged. That was the least of his problems. "So we dismantle it."

"If we push it, we can make the town in five hours, little longer if we have to travel at night," said Clark as a plan formulated in his mind. "Enough time to dismantle the *laager*."

Archie knew enough Afrikaans words to know he meant the camp. "That's a waste of manpower . . ." Archie began.

Clark held up his hand to cut him off. "What if we tell the authorities and Jane comes walkin' out of there all smilin'? Then we get arrested if they find out about this place and you'll be seein' your daughter from behind bars—if you're lucky! Or what if she comes back to find her dad mauled to death because he ran into the bush unprepared, eh?"

Robbie could see Archie was wrestling with his conscience. He wanted Archie to shout and complain, then crash out into the jungle to pursue Jane, but he was taking Clark's advice to heart.

Clark pressed on. "Mister David led a search party out as far as they could, and they didn't find nothin'." Archie's face looked gray, etched with worry. "That's a good sign. Means she's alive and mobile. Also means we can't just walk out there and expect to find her today. We've got four hours to sunset then we're stuck.

"Be realistic, an aerial search is impractical in the jungle. We might be able to get some help from rangers, but it'll take too long, and they won't be able to do much more than us, so I don't think it's worth the hassle. I say some fellas stay here, just in case she returns, while we take a team into the green to look for her at first light. Gives us enough time to gather supplies and weapons tonight. Don't know about you, mate, but if Tafari or another bunch of loggers have got her, I don't wanna face a bunch of crazy armed idiots with just a few sticks!"

Archie weighed up his slim options and nodded.

"I want my daughter back, Clark. That's all that matters."

Clark squeezed his friend's shoulder. "We'll find her, mate. We will."

Robbie had listened for long enough.

"So that's it? You're just going to wait until tomorrow to go looking for her?"

Clark sighed. "No. We're going to organize a proper search for her rather than just run aimlessly about."

Robbie shook his head. He knew it was futile to try to persuade them to leave tonight. He stormed off across the encampment. All around, workers were gathered in small groups quietly talking. Nobody was doing anything productive.

"What are you doing?" screamed Robbie. "Jane's lost out there. She's in trouble! We should be looking for her!"

The workers stared at Robbie with grim faces. Nobody moved. Esmée sat in the shade of the school shack, her eyes averted as Robbie ran over to her.

"You agree with me, right? We need to be looking for Jane!"

Esmée looked at him with tearful eyes. She had been crying for some time. She didn't answer. Clark ran up behind Robbie and grabbed his arm, twisting him around. He was furious and the anger in his voice came out as a sharp hiss.

"What the hell d'you think you're doin'?"

"Trying to do something, unlike you!" snarled Robbie as he tried to shake Clark off. The big man's grip was too strong. "Get off me!"

"You listen to me, Robert. This is a serious situation and the last thing we need is anyone creatin' panic!"

"I'm not panicking, I'm trying to find Jane!"

"You're not helpin'! Listen to me. Every man here knows if we call the authorities on this then we can all end up behind bars. You included. And believe me, you really don't wanna see the inside of a Congolese prison." He jerked a thumb toward the workers. "If they got wind that's what we were doin' then they'd run. Hear me? They'd run to save their own skins because to them, this is just another job. Without 'em we have no one to help look for Jane."

Robbie didn't want to hear that. While some of the loggers were taciturn or didn't speak English, the majority were fun to be around. "That's not true . . ."

"'Course it is! Now they all like the girl, and they'll help search, but we can't go spookin' 'em. And what if we got found out? You think you'd ever see your girlfriend again?"

"She's not my girlfriend," snapped Robbie. "She's a friend—more like a sister! And to me family is important."

Robbie tried to pull away from Clark's grip, but it was too strong.

"Really? If family's so important then I don't suppose you mind bein' deported back to the States where they will ask some really probin' questions into your family life." Clark didn't know the details of why Robbie had fled, but had his suspicions. He released Robbie's arm, satisfied his message was getting through. "Not to mention what Tafari would do to any of us if we go bargin' in there accusin' them of kidnappin'. We have to handle this carefully. Tell me this is gettin' through to you."

Robbie looked around. Everybody was staring at them.

"I get it," muttered Robbie.

"I wanna see her back as much as you. I've known her since she was a *pikkie*. Archie's my best mate. If you care about any of us, you'll do as I say."

Robbie nodded, but refused to look Clark in the eye.

"Good. Now let's sort this mess out."

He headed back to Archie's shack. Robbie called after him, not too loud as he had no desire to gain any more attention.

"Clark. If it was me out there . . . would you do the same thing?"

Clark nodded. "Archie would have the sense to calm me down. We'd do exactly the same thing."

Robbie nodded thoughtfully then smiled. His mind was made up.

As soon as he could slip away unnoticed he would search for Jane alone.

• • •

Jane's stomach rumbled so loudly it got the attention of a young black-back that had clambered up the trail and lain next to the aircraft to bathe in the sun. The gorilla made low grumbling noises in return and rolled onto its chest to study Jane. One hand cradled its chin, the other idly scratched his prominent sagittal crest that made the top of his head appear almost egg-shaped.

The ape grumbled again and Jane felt he was waiting for an answer. She imitated the noise as best she could. It seemed to satisfy the animal, which rolled over, picking at some vine leaves. A smaller gorilla bounded onto his chest and the two began hooting as they tickled one another in a play-fight.

Despite the playful behavior, Jane was all too aware she was in the presence of wild animals and was too petrified to move. Tarzan had disappeared without a word after he had eaten. The sight of him eating the pig raw got Jane's imagination running wild. Was he some kind of cannibal? Had he eaten the aircraft's crew? And was she next on the menu?

She tried to blank that thought. Tarzan had attacked the lioness . . . what kind of maniac attacks a lion with his bare hands?

No. He'd attacked the lioness to save her and had brought her back here to tend to her wounds. She had no reason to be afraid of him; she just had to convince herself of that. But the image of Tarzan kneeling over the pig, his mouth and hands covered in fresh blood, refused to budge from her mind.

Since Tarzan had shouted at the silverback, Kerchak, there had been no more hostile behavior toward her. Kerchak had moved further up the slope and sat with a small group of females.

Tana kept close, and Jane got the impression the ape was making sure she didn't get into any trouble. Karnath soon tired and fell asleep in his mother's arms. Jane was surprised to feel a pang of jealousy at the close family bond.

Without a watch Jane couldn't tell how much time had passed. The sun had definitely moved from over one peak to another, but it could have taken ten minutes or three hours. Her stomach continued to growl, and the apes sauntered around her as if she had always been a permanent fixture.

She began to feel an overwhelming sense of abandonment. Why hadn't anybody come looking for her? Then again, maybe they had. Even she didn't know where *here* was and her initial expectations of an aerial search were snuffed out the moment she looked back at the crashed airplane. Had anybody come looking for that? What happened to the crew and passengers? Were their remains still inside the plane? She didn't recall seeing anything when she woke, but then again she hadn't been looking for them. Had Tarzan eaten—

A loud thump jolted her out of her dark imaginings. Tarzan had landed on top of the aircraft. Jane looked around—how had he done that? There were only trees on the side of the mountain. Surely she would have heard him approach. As Tarzan jumped down to the ground she saw that he was cradling something in one arm. She hoped it wasn't another dead animal.

Tarzan slowly approached her, his eyes fixed on hers as if he still didn't know if she was friend or foe. He edged closer and scraped a bowl into the earth with one hand, then dropped the catch that was tucked in his other arm.

Jane expected something disgusting but was relieved to see that Tarzan had brought her fruits, nuts, and a chunk of mushroom. Jane couldn't identify anything specific except the large green banana-like plantain. As she picked up the fruit she yelped at the sight of several large green crickets and thick caterpillars trapped underneath.

"Urgh!" She tried to shake the insect off. Tarzan watched her with a frown, and his hand shot out and caught the cricket before it dropped to the ground. He held it up for her to see, then popped it in his mouth. Jane watched in revulsion as Tarzan munched on the insect.

"*Nesen.* Good."

"You . . . you've still got a leg . . ." She indicated to the side of her mouth. Tarzan evidently understood as his tongue darted out to lick the stray cricket leg. "That's revolting."

Jane's stomach rumbled again. Tarzan's brow knitted together with concern, and he gently shoved the plantain closer to Jane, an indication she should eat it. With a sigh, Jane gripped the stem and tugged—but the sturdy plantain wouldn't open. She tried again, but the fruit remained sealed.

"It's not ripe enough," she muttered.

Karnath rolled around the foliage next to Jane and eyed the food with curiosity. The little ape took the plantain from her hand, held it by the stem and gently squeezed the opposite end of the fruit. The plantain's skin split effortlessly, revealing the green fruit. To her amazement, Karnath handed the plantain back.

Jane bit into it. She'd had plantain almost every day at the camp, but Esmée had taken pains to cook and flavor it. Raw, it tasted like raw potato, but she was hungry and with the alternative being dead pig or bugs, she closed her eyes and pretended it was a sweet banana. After the first few mouthfuls she became resigned to the bland taste and finished it off quickly. She was still hungry but ignored the fat wriggling caterpillar Tarzan offered her, and instead took the large piece of fungus. She sniffed it. It smelt fine, but she was all too aware of the many toxic fungi in the jungle. She glanced at Tarzan, regretfully seeing the tail end of a caterpillar being sucked between his lips. Tarzan nodded encouragingly at the fungus, so Jane took a deep breath and bit into it. The texture felt odd in her mouth, but it tasted like a sweet mushroom. It would be better fried, but she couldn't complain.

She finished the mushroom and a second plantain under Tarzan's watchful gaze. He never attempted to speak or interrupt her. When she finished, she was full but still far from relaxed. Tarzan didn't seem in a rush to start a conversation so Jane tried.

"Thanks for the food."

Tarzan seemed to be staring through her and it took a moment for

Jane to realize he was looking at her hair. Maybe he hadn't seen blonde hair before. She self-consciously wrapped it into a ponytail.

"I should be going back. My dad must be going crazy." Tarzan made no indication he understood. "You know? Back to my camp? Where I live?" Nothing seemed to register. "I need to go *home*."

"Home!" Tarzan barked the word and nodded. "Home."

Jane felt a flush of relief and nodded enthusiastically. "Yes, home. You can show me the way home."

Tarzan sprang to his feet and walked to the edge of the cliff, gesturing to Jane to follow. She reluctantly joined him, trying to ignore the sheer drop below. Karnath trotted over to Tarzan and leapt into his arms. He held him with one hand and pointed across the vista.

"Home."

There was nothing but trees reaching all the way to the horizon. The apes below were either eating or playfully chasing one another. There were no signs of civilization.

"*Mangani* are family," said Tarzan pointing to the apes. Karnath jumped from his hands and clung to Jane's leg. She tried not to yelp as she wrestled the irrational fear that the gorilla was about to bite her. Instead it just looked at her with big brown eyes and bared its teeth in a rictus of a smile.

"Home," repeated Tarzan. Jane took a deep breath to subdue her frustration. This would be more difficult than she'd anticipated.

• • •

"Dammit!" yelled Robbie as the machete twisted from his hand and dropped to the ground—narrowly missing his foot. His arm ached from sweeping the blade through the dense foliage as he dutifully followed the overflowing brook for a mile or so before it joined a river. He'd studied how Mister David hacked through thick vegetation and had used the machete himself on many occasions to trim the logs they had hewn down. But alone it was tough going. Several times Robbie had had to stop himself from wildly swinging the blade with his free hand outstretched, which felt a more natural motion. He'd heard many stories over campfires of people who had inadvertently slashed their own hand off.

Robbie sat on some rocks that sloped into the river. He was unsure if this was the same tributary they floated the logs down, as it looked unfamiliar and there were several nearby. After traveling for two hours he was already exhausted, so took a long gulp of water from his canteen to quench his thirst. In his rush to get away he had only packed one water canteen and he was beginning to realize that was a mistake.

He'd made the pretense of helping Esmée load the kitchen supplies into a crate, just in case they had to suddenly dismantle the camp, while secretly stealing provisions for his rescue attempt. Archie and Clark had gathered the loggers and were talking through their plan, but all Robbie could see was their total lack of action. He'd taken a heavy waterproof flashlight, a canvas sheet, firelighters, and a machete from a set of open supply crates. As an afterthought he stole a pistol from Clark's cabin. He'd fired a rifle before, taking part in impromptu shooting ranges the workers would sometimes set up to relieve the boredom. He thought a handgun wouldn't be much different and felt safer with it.

The first half of the trek had been easy and had already taken him farther than Mister David's initial circle of the area. All he had to do was follow the flow downstream and look for any likely places Jane could have washed ashore, or been forced ashore by her kidnappers. Robbie was quickly coming to the conclusion that Tafari's rebels had nothing to do with Jane's disappearance. For one, he was heading in the opposite direction from the rebels' camp. Perhaps Jane had just got lost on her own? But in that case who had attacked the camp?

That meant she was out here, all alone.

"Alone," he mumbled. The word stuck in his throat. *Sophie had been alone when . . .*

He shunned the bad memories and desperately tried to think of a happy time with his sister. He recalled a perfect memory—ice-skating in Central Park one Christmas.

Festive decorations strung between trees; the open-air rink was filled with people enjoying themselves. Sophie teaching him how to skate and giggling every time he fell over. Her laughter was so infectious that he couldn't help laughing too . . .

That was the last time he'd heard her laugh. He pushed the memory aside. The rocks he sat on were the first place he'd come across where Jane could have washed ashore, but there was no trace she had done so. A fragment of doubt began to gnaw at Robbie. Maybe Clark was right, maybe blindly searching for Jane was a stupid idea.

"Pull yourself together," he muttered. The word *maybe* often led to inaction and procrastination. It was what had led him to endure misery in New York. If he had acted sooner, maybe things would have been very different.

A branch cracked.

The crack was one of the most chilling sounds to hear while sitting alone in one of the most remote places on earth. Robbie realized he was completely exposed to whatever was approaching.

His hand slowly went to the pistol poking from his pocket. He twisted his neck a fraction as foliage gently rustled.

Then something stepped out just behind him. It was a small deer standing one-and-a-half feet tall with brown-gray fur and short horns—a cute-looking Peters's duiker. Robbie had seen them brought back to Karibu Mji for food. The timid animal sniffed the air and stared at Robbie. Robbie hadn't moved for some time, so the duiker didn't see him as a threat. It approached the water's edge and began to drink, keeping one cautious eye on Robbie as it did so.

Robbie didn't want to scare the little guy. He was glad of the company and the reassurance that not everything in the jungle was out to kill him.

The water suddenly erupted as something darted for the duiker. In the white froth, Robbie could only see a massive pair of crocodile jaws clamp down on the deer before it could react. The reptile vanished with its prize as quickly as it had appeared. Robbie didn't stay to watch—he was sprinting through the undergrowth as fast as possible.

• • •

Despite her protests, Tarzan led Jane down the steep trail to the lake. She found it difficult, pain shooting down her leg from the wound, but Tarzan made no effort to assist her. They passed several gorillas who watched them with interest but didn't react to the stranger in their midst. Tarzan would greet each new gorilla with a throaty grumble, which they replied to. Jane realized it meant "everything is OK," but she still kept close to Tarzan, not wishing to be left alone with the brutes.

"You have to understand, I need to get to *my* home!" She had been complaining the entire way to the lake, but Tarzan had ignored her. They reached the lakeshore at the base of the waterfall and Tarzan gestured across the water.

"Very nice," said Jane without looking. "I know you can understand a little of what I say . . ."

Tarzan gently gripped her chin, forcing her to look across the lake. He was too strong for her to resist. She was about to continue speaking when she saw it.

The sun was dipping below the caldera edge, sending golden rays across the lake, and silhouetting the gorillas drinking from the bank. Across the lake, in the last vestiges of the setting sun, a dozen odd-looking deer swam in the water—water chevrotain, she recalled from the pictures Esmée had shown her—their mouse-like heads ducking to eat submerged weeds. From the plateau the view had taken her breath away, but down here it was even more stunning.

She took a step forward, her hand brushing tall curling orchids; their sweet smell overwhelmed her senses. The bank was covered with vibrant flora, clinging to every available surface.

"It's . . . it's beautiful," she finally admitted. It had certainly made her forget the pain in her leg.

She looked at Tarzan and saw he was frowning and staring at her intently. Jane felt as if he was trying to tell her something but lacked the vocabulary.

They sat on the edge of the lake watching the sun slowly sink behind the mountains. Chirping filled the air as familiar crimson-rumped waxbills darted to snatch flies and colorful butterflies made their last rounds on the flowers.

As the shadows reached them, Tarzan finally spoke.

"Dark soon," said Tarzan. "Dangerous for Jane."

Jane had come to the same conclusion so had decided not to pursue the matter of getting home. She followed him and the straggling gorillas back up the track to the aircraft. Some of the females and younger gorillas sat in the trees, bending branches into mattresses in the safety of the boughs. Larger silverbacks and blackbacks contented themselves with making their nests on the ground.

Watching the animals bed down, Jane was surprised to feel safe.

Then the image of Tarzan, his hands and mouth smeared in blood as he ate raw flesh came back to her and she shivered at the thought of spending the night so close to a killer.

7

A billion insects chirped through the darkness and every single one of them was out to get Robbie. Or at least that's what he thought as he huddled in the limb of a crabwood tree. He had tried sleeping on the ground, next to the small fire he had lit with deadwood, but the sounds of creeping bugs drove him to the tree where he thought he'd be safe from predators.

He'd eaten an energy bar and a handful of trail mix, determined to be sensible with his rations, but he was still hungry. He closed his eyes and tried to concentrate on the individual sounds around him. The rhythmic chirps of frogs, the high-pitched sawing of crickets, an occasional deep grunt in the canopy from a monkey, the flap of leathery bat wings as a colony of them hunted across the jungle and the incessant whine of mosquitoes as they nibbled his neck and ears. Archie had provided malaria tablets to his team, knowing it was the main disease likely to kill them out here. Robbie couldn't remember the last time he'd taken them. Not that that would keep away the tsetse flies that carried the deadly African sleeping sickness. In his rush to find Jane, he'd forgotten to bring a bug spray or mosquito net.

He sat miserably in the tree, not daring to move in case he fell out.

His left leg was already numb as he curled up as tightly as possible and blanked out the din around him. He just hoped there were no snakes. In this dense jungle he wouldn't know about it until it was too late.

Then, as if to further his misery, the heavens opened up with a raging torrent. Thunder reverberated across the valley, and Robbie began to doubt the wisdom of sheltering in a tree during a thunderstorm; he thought he would be a magnet for lightning.

He shivered, wrapping his arms around his numb legs. He was sure he could hear the gentle hiss of a snake.

• • •

Archie watched the jagged lightning fork across the horizon, but the storm was still far off. Fear of another kidnapping gripped the camp when it was discovered that Robbie Canler was missing too. Clark and Mister David had searched the area in the fading light and had found Robbie's footprints heading into the jungle.

Archie had felt a twinge of guilt that Robbie had blundered off to look for his daughter while he had done nothing.

"You'll call me a hypocrite since I made Robbie keep studyin'," said Clark, drinking a whisky-laced coffee in front of the fire, "but the lad's not as savvy as he thinks he is."

"And you think Jane is?"

"If Jane's been taken by Tafari, that's one thing. If Robbie goes in guns blazin' then he'll get them both killed."

Archie nodded grimly. Another flash of lightning ripped through the sky. The rain increased in ferocity; fat drops clattered off the corrugated-iron roof sounding more like hailstones.

"As soon as the storm passes, we leave," said Archie without looking at Clark for confirmation.

"And the camp?" Clark asked as innocently as he could, indicating the camp around them. Everything both men had was tied up with the business.

"To hell with the camp," hissed Archie. "We find them, then we worry about all this!" Clark nodded in understanding. "Esmée is making packs and Mister David is organizing the men. We'll leave some here on guard."

"And how much will that cost?" Clark knew the men would only risk life and limb in a search party if they were being paid handsomely. The dangers of the jungle were great.

Archie laughed cheerlessly. "More than we've got right now."

The storm raged and the two men didn't say another word as they waited for the chance to begin the search.

• • •

Nervous grunts came from the trees as the thunder ferociously boomed through the mountains. It woke Jane from the deepest sleep she could remember. Tarzan had brought her some fresh branches and laid them on the floor of the fuselage as a mattress, which was surprisingly comfortable. Then he had left as night encroached. The grunts from the band outside felt reassuring, and the rain battering her shelter was soothing.

Now that she was feeling safe, she allowed her mind to wander. Her first thought was of how she would get back to camp. That would be something she would try to communicate to Tarzan in the morning. Thinking about her strange savior, she reflected on who he was and how he came to be living with wild apes. She desperately wanted to search the aircraft for clues to Tarzan's identity, but the darkness within was absolute. She tried to stand, but felt a wave of dizziness that forced her to lie back down. She clutched her head wound. Tarzan had done his best to tend it, but she was certain he was no medic, although he had done an excellent job with her leg. She wondered what the tiny beads were that held the wound together. She'd never seen stitching like it, and she'd seen a lot when her father had been a doctor. Where had Tarzan learned that skill?

Tiredness washed over her, and her eyelids felt leaden. She tried to combat the fatigue when Tana poked her head into the shelter, little Karnath clinging to her. Both were wet from the downpour and looked agitated as thunder rumbled again. They edged into the artificial cave and settled down at the foot of Jane's nest. Despite their presence, Jane could no longer stay awake and drifted back to sleep.

It was dawn, and Robbie had barely slept. The storm had curtailed, but the rain continued. And he was wet through to his skin. He climbed from the tree, falling the last seven feet because his leg was still numb. He hadn't brought a change of clothes and wondered if it was possible to get hypothermia in the tropical climate. His neck itched from the numerous insect bites and it was a battle of will not to scratch them. He decided to leave breakfast until he had dried out, so grabbed his pack and continued following the river.

Hours passed as he hacked his way through the verdure and he began mumbling half-forgotten lyrics to spur him on. Just as he was starting to doubt that Jane could have possibly drifted this far down-river, the bushes cleared and he found himself on the banks of three converging tributaries that merged into one huge river that carved through the jungle.

"DAMMIT!" he screamed to whoever would listen. Several parrots cawed in reply.

Robbie slumped on the riverbank, feeling disheartened. He felt stupid. The wilderness was too vast to track Jane down singlehandedly. She was still out there, alone, possibly injured. Or worse. And so was he.

The unwelcome image of his sister barged into his mind's eye. *Lying in her bed; eyes closed, skin pale, her body horribly thin. She was dead. That's how he had found her. Dead . . .*

Robbie's fingers clenched as he shook with rage and grief at the unwelcome memory. If only he'd reacted quicker. If only he'd spoken out. If only . . .

He wiped the tears away from his eyes, and suddenly noticed something on the opposite bank: a swatch of blue. It was such a strong color against the browns, yellows, and greens that it stood out as artificial.

It was enough to suddenly give him hope that Jane had indeed come this way. Any clues to which direction she had taken lay across the river. All Robbie had to do was get over there.

The muddy river waters flowed swiftly, some branches zipped by while others were caught in powerful eddies as the three rivers clashed together. Robbie was a strong swimmer and judged his options. If he swam from farther upstream he calculated he should be able to cross without the currents making him overshoot his intended landing area, but it was a gamble.

That's when he noticed the shapes in the water. What he had previously assumed were rocks suddenly submerged, only to reappear a minute later with the twitch of an ear.

"Hippos . . . great," he said aloud. There were six of them, four adults and two babies, and they showed no intention of leaving the area they wallowed in.

He looked around for an alternative route. The arcing trees formed a leafy tunnel over the narrowest point of the river and the branches looked sturdy enough to support his weight.

Robbie secured his backpack and approached the foot of a tree. The gnarled bark provided plenty of handholds and his ascent was made easier by dozens of low-hanging branches. Ten feet up his hand cut through a column of ants. He quickly pulled his fingers away before the large-headed soldier ants could bite him. He traced the line of ants up to a large mass in the crook of the tree that appeared to move as if alive. Climbing a little higher, Robbie could see that it *was* alive. It was a bivouac three feet in diameter constructed from the bodies of a hundred thousand ants all clinging together. Army ants poured out of their living shelter with renewed vigor when they detected Robbie's scent and veered toward him.

Robbie quickened his pace toward the thick bough that bent over the river, but the ants were quicker and massed in their thousands. Robbie had expected them to make a terrifying scuttling noise, but their silence was more ominous. He could already see the massive heads and powerful pincers of the soldier ants as they got uncomfortably near. These ants had been known to kill humans, and Robbie couldn't think of a more painful death.

He scrambled farther up the tree as the first of the ants crawled onto his sleeve. He couldn't risk letting go of the branch to swat them. Instead, he gritted his teeth as the powerful jaws pinched through his jacket, and hauled himself into the crook of the branch. He brushed ants off his sleeve and pants, receiving nasty nips to his fingers. The swarm continued advancing, forcing Robbie to run across the branch, his arms windmilling to keep his balance. The ants relentlessly pursued as he ran over the river, the branch sagging from his weight with every step.

Robbie fought to catch his balance and resisted the terrible itching he felt all over his body. The ants followed along the limb, which was now sagging so much it threatened to drop him in the water where the hippos bathed.

From the ground, the branches of the tree on the opposite bank had appeared to mesh together to form a natural bridge. But now that he was closer he could see that it had been an illusion and the sturdy branches he needed to get to were a tantalizing seven feet away. He would have to jump. The bough behind him was seething with ants, so there was no going back.

Robbie took a deep breath and jumped.

He sailed through the air, arms and legs flailing until the thick branches whipped at his face. He blindly reached out for purchase, his arms ripping leaves and twigs. He felt his stomach lurch as he dropped—then suddenly stopped as his hand snagged a tough branch that supported his weight. His arm felt as though it would be ripped from its socket but he refused to let go. His legs dangled over the hippopotamuses that circled in the water as they watched the intruder above.

With a grunt of effort, Robbie heaved himself up onto the stout branch and wrapped his arms and legs around it for safety. He lay there and caught his breath. He'd done it! He examined the stinging welts on his fingers caused by the ants. They already looked swollen and he cursed himself for forgetting to bring any medical supplies with him.

Without any further drama, Robbie lowered himself to the ground and ran across to the blue fragment. It was a torn swatch of denim. A splattering of blood and the ragged tear suggested an animal had torn it off. A few feet away, Jane's phone lay in the mud. There was no doubt that she had passed this way and was injured. He took his pack off to put the phone somewhere dry, then turned and froze.

A baby hippopotamus had stepped onto the bank and was watching him curiously. Even the baby was the size of a large desk.

"Easy," soothed Robbie in his calmest voice.

The noise startled the hippo, which mewed loudly, drawing the attention of its mother. The hippo surged from the water like a torpedo. Robbie was stunned by the size and speed of the beast. He sprinted as fast as he could in the opposite direction as the hippo plowed through vegetation in pursuit, its huge mouth hinged open revealing dagger-like teeth.

Robbie's lungs were bursting as he ran for his life, hurdling trailing tree roots and ducking sturdy branches—all of which splintered apart as the animal charged. He vaulted over a boulder, limbs pumping hard as he fled, before he became aware that the angry parent had given up the chase. Robbie dropped to his knees, exhausted. He cursed the jungle as loudly as he could, wondering what other dangers it could possibly throw at him.

He wouldn't have long to wait.

• • •

Two hours before dawn the storm had abated enough for Mister David to declare the search party should move out.

Archie and Clark had slept in fits and starts but had not spoken a further word. They didn't need to, as they had been friends since university and had taken the rough with the smooth. Archie had helped Clark through many dubious legal situations he always found himself in when circumnavigating the globe, and Clark had been there when Archie's wife had left him, taking every penny he owned and destroying his life and career. Clark was driven by money and it was no surprise to Archie that he couldn't shake off the financial implications of closing the camp. Archie knew Clark wasn't putting Jane and Robbie in second place; it was just his abrasive manner made it seem that way.

Clark didn't trust any of the loggers enough to send them to the town for help in case they said the wrong thing—he had hoped to send Robbie or go himself. He had ordered nine men to guard the camp while six volunteers joined Mister David, Archie, and Clark in the search party, armed with hunting rifles. Archie slung his shoulder holster on, loading up his revolver, and Clark, discovering his handgun was missing, strapped a combat knife to his calf. They both knew you could never be too prepared in the wilderness. A raft, used when they floated the logs downstream, had been deflated and rolled into a pack, and Esmée had prepared enough provisions to last several days.

Their powerful flashlights easily found the trail that Robbie had hacked through the jungle and they followed it as swiftly as they could. Boots squelched through mud and branches cracked underfoot. They weren't worried about making noise, as it would hopefully scare off any predators waiting for them in the darkness.

• • •

Jane tried to move her pillow, but it didn't budge. Her cheeks felt warm against the softness . . .

Her eyes flicked open and she took a moment to decide whether she should panic or not. She prodded the greasy fur she'd slept against and Tana moved aside. The gorilla didn't seem to mind and concentrated on chewing a piece of bark. Karnath was delicately grooming Jane's hair, occasionally finding something that it ate. Jane dreaded to think what insects may have crawled into her hair and thought it best not to worry about it.

She sat up and was surprised to see more fruits had been delivered. She was glad her host had got the message and not brought insects or raw flesh.

Jane stood, and found her leg looked much better, although the wound hurt more than the previous day. Perhaps Tarzan's healing had included some anesthetic that had worn off? She fought a dizzy spell and closed her eyes.

"I'm OK," she assured herself. "I can do this."

She took several steps unaided before she was forced to lean against the remains of a passenger seat. While she rested she noticed something poking from under the seat. Curious, she reached down and retrieved a faded blue helmet with large white letters: UN. She'd seen them before on the news, worn by United Nations peacekeeping soldiers. She replaced it and examined the rest of the aircraft.

From the dirt and rust, it was obvious that the plane had been in the jungle for many years. Her initial search found nothing of interest in the main cabin and the cockpit also lacked any clues. A moldy leather case stowed next to the pilot's seat bore the legend: GREYSTOKE. Was that a person? A company? The paper contents of the case had long since rotted. The windshield had shattered on impact and the glass lenses on the instruments were either missing or cracked. She was thankful the bodies of the pilots had been removed and she mused that it was possible that they had survived the crash and walked out.

Jane ventured outside, enjoying the fine rain on her face. The gorillas had already dispersed across the mountainside so she cautiously examined the outside of the plane. The tail number had all but faded and was illegible under moss and rust. The rear cargo hatch was partially open and the rusted hinges grated as Jane opened it further. She jumped as a large yellow tarantula scuttled out, but her curiosity overrode any fear she felt.

Inside the dark hold were three crates. One had split, its contents spread over the hold, but the others appeared to be still sealed. Jane could just see a suitcase beyond them. The spilt crate appeared to be old and contained rusted scientific equipment wrapped in moldy foam packing chips, all of which was spilled across the floor.

She felt somebody was watching her and spun around. Tarzan stood on a rock, eyeing her suspiciously, his eyes darting from her to the open cargo door, then back again.

"I was curious," said Jane. "Um, interested to know more about you."

Tarzan watched her intently, but offered no words.

"Did you see this plane crash? Where are you from?" The most obvious answer suddenly hit her, but it was too unbelievable to vocalize—*had he been on the plane when it crashed?* She'd previously assumed he had stumbled across the aircraft and it looked like this had crashed well over a decade ago. "Where did you learn English?"

"D'Arnot," came the reply. Jane frowned. She hadn't heard of such a place, but it had got the mysterious man talking.

"D'Arnot. Never heard of it. Is it far?"

Tarzan shook his head. There was a look of sadness in his eyes, but it was so fleeting Jane didn't know if it was a trick of the light. She wondered if there was a radio at D'Arnot. She was grasping at straws but she had to get word to her father.

"Can you take me to D'Arnot?"

Tarzan looked at her long and hard, then finally nodded. Jane felt a tremor of excitement at the thought she might finally be reunited with her dad.

"Now?" she added when Tarzan made no move.

Tarzan crossed to a tree and motioned her over. Before she could reach him he scampered up the trunk in several bounds. He was quick and Jane couldn't see the route he had climbed.

"Hey? Where you going?"

Tarzan appeared through the upper branches.

"Come!"

"Up there? I thought we were going to D'Arnot?"

Tarzan jumped down—bouncing off two branches as he zigzagged to the lowest bough. He moved with swift assurance that astonished Jane. He reached for her hand.

"I'm not climbing any tree!" She folded her arms to emphasize her point.

Tarzan suddenly grabbed Jane's wrist and plucked her upward with immense strength. Jane shrieked as he pulled her onto the branch he stood on, then grabbed her around the waist like a ragdoll. Jane would have beaten his chest, but Tarzan had pinned both her arms by her sides.

"What are you doing?" she screamed. "Let me dow—"

The word was sucked from her lips as Tarzan vaulted up, using one hand to pull them to the next branch, muscular legs carrying them higher. Tarzan moved without thought, using one tree branch to bounce to another in rapid succession. It reminded Jane of the acrobatic parkour free runners who used to attend her school, back when she had a life.

Within seconds they had reached the top of the tree and Tarzan dropped her lightly onto a branch.

Jane was fuming. "Are you crazy?" She had vague recollections of moving rapidly through the treetops when Tarzan had first saved her, but had put that down to a hallucination. "Take me back down!"

She made the mistake of looking down as she said it. They must have been forty feet off the ground and the tree leaned out over the plateau offering a head-spinning drop of another 130 feet. Jane was usually good with heights, but standing on the narrow limb made her legs buckle. Tarzan caught her before she could fall.

"I don't want to be up here! You said we're going to D'Arnot."

Tarzan's grip was like iron. He didn't waver in the slightest. His piercing eyes sparkled mischievously.

"D'Arnot, this way." He pointed across the jungle.

Jane didn't follow his finger in case it triggered another bout of vertigo. "That's great. How are we going to get there?"

Tarzan effortlessly pulled Jane's arms around his neck and firmly linked them.

"Hold. Tight."

A sense of foreboding overwhelmed Jane as she began to suspect Tarzan really was the maniac she had initially assumed. He straightened up—a simple act that swept Jane off her feet. She dangled behind him, not daring to let go.

"Are you crazy?" she yelled as Tarzan sprinted to the edge of the branch—and jumped.

8

Robbie strained to hear the river—that at least would give him a direction to walk in. The blind sprint from the rampaging hippopotamus had confounded his sense of direction. After cautiously retracing his steps he failed to locate the river, which meant he wasn't retracing his steps at all. Clark had drummed into him the importance of leaving a trail to follow back and now Robbie understood just how vital that was.

The jungle floor had been gently climbing for the last couple of hours as he followed the animal trails that provided the path of least resistance. Now the trails had become steeper. A clearing in the jungle offered a tantalizing view—he was walking up the flanks of a ponderous mountain, the top of which was smothered in cloud.

"You've got to be kidding me," he said to the jungle at large.

He couldn't recall seeing mountains from the camp, and reason dictated that the river would be at the foot of the mountain so he made the decision to turn around and walk back. The very notion filled him with despair, not for his own safety, but for how he had let Jane down.

Before he started retracing his steps he found a boulder to sit on and pulled out his trail mix, the only thing he had eaten all day. His mind drifted to his first days in Africa. What had he expected to find? A new life certainly, but *this*? He shook his head sadly. Running away had been an impulsive act, just like searching for Jane. But he was impetuous, that's why he'd left New York far behind. His mother's drinking problem had blinded her to the actions of their abusive step-father. And Sophie . . . a chill ran through him when he thought of his sister.

The snap of branches brought him back to the present; something was approaching. He ducked behind the boulder. Whatever it was, it was big and it was advancing from the other side of the clearing.

Bushes swayed as more branches cracked—and the largest man Robbie had ever seen stepped out of the undergrowth, a curved kukri in one hand and an automatic rifle in the other. Five more men followed him into the clearing, all wearing sweat-stained khaki shirts and caps and equally well armed. They spoke fragments of French and Kikongo, which Robbie had heard in the villages, but English was the common tongue amongst them.

Robbie assumed they were rangers and, while relieved, wondered what excuse he could give for being lost in the jungle without betraying his friends.

The men looked around the glade and started arguing, buying Robbie more time to think of an excuse as he eavesdropped. But he soon realized that these men weren't rangers, they were rebels.

"Next man to complain gets a bullet to the head!" snarled the lead brute.

"Come on, Bapoto, you know this is a waste of time," muttered a scrawny man who sported burn marks on his neck.

Bapoto hefted the point of his kukri close to the man's chest.

"Shut your face, Oudry, or I'll finish the job the fire started!" he snarled.

"Easy!" said Oudry fearfully, his hands raised to placate Bapoto. "I meant they're just a bunch of loggers."

Robbie pressed himself to the ground as low as he could. The boulder and tall grass was the only cover he had; the distance to the dense jungle was too far for him to reach without being spotted. He cursed the bad luck that had led them to cross paths in the sprawling wilderness. He shouldn't have used the animal trails—they were the pathways used by both predators and prey and that was asking for trouble. And now he'd found it.

Bapoto sheathed his kukri and slung his rifle over a broad shoulder before taking a long swig from his water bottle. He poured a little over his forehead before he spoke again.

"Tafari wants a message delivered, and that's what we do."

Robbie's pulse quickened. So, they'd attacked the camp and kidnapped Jane just to send a message? He fought the compulsion to attack the men right now—he wouldn't stand a chance against them. He controlled his anger—maybe if he followed them he would be led to Jane.

Bapoto spat on the ground. "If they're dumb enough to try an' sabotage our jeeps, then we put them outta business, *comprenez*?"

Robbie was suddenly confused—*their* jeeps? They were having problems with a saboteur too?

"Might not have been them, Bapoto," cautioned another man. "You know that."

"*Negoogunogumbar*," muttered a fourth man.

"Don't mention that name out here," warned Bapoto. He looked around the trees with genuine fear. "It ain't no spirit."

"You sure of that?" asked Oudry, glad to see the lieutenant was frightened of something. "'Cause we're about to go to war over it."

"Not war," growled Bapoto. "Just a warnin'."

"Could have delivered a warning by driving there," mumbled Oudry.

"We want to take 'em by surprise! They'd see us coming on the main track, so we take the long path and we don't whine about it!"

Robbie gasped. They were heading toward Karibu Mji for an attack. He mentally put the pieces together. The rebels had been attacked and thought it was the loggers . . . which meant there was a third party involved. It also meant the rebels hadn't kidnapped Jane . . .

Bapoto had stopped talking and was looking around the clearing as if he'd heard Robbie. Robbie ducked and prayed he hadn't been spotted. No sound came from the men and he could only imagine they were all peering in his direction.

Grass rustled. Somebody was approaching. He could hear the soft squelch of heavy boots on the damp ground. Then they stopped—and Robbie realized he was holding his breath.

"Get movin'!" growled Bapoto. "Want to reach 'em before dawn tomorrow!"

Robbie peeked over the rock. Bapoto had walked half the distance toward him, but was now turned to face his men. With a collective groan the rebels continued across the glade at an angle to Robbie. He kept himself low, ducking again at the last moment when Bapoto turned and scanned the clearing before disappearing into the trees.

So the rebels hadn't kidnapped Jane; that much was clear. So was she lost? Had she already arrived back at the camp? Or was a mysterious third party responsible for abducting her, the same saboteurs who had attacked Karibu Mji and Tafari's camp? Robbie shook his head. The rebels and the loggers shared the same problem but neither realized it.

With a heavy heart he knew it was time to abandon his search for Jane. He had to follow the guerrillas back to Karibu Mji and warn his friends before violence broke out.

• • •

Their speed was incalculable. Jane tried to close her eyes to blot out the death-defying leaps, but couldn't. Colorful birds shot out of their path as Tarzan rushed through their domain and the occasional bright green or red feather would catch in Jane's hair.

Tarzan landed in the treetops that clung to the side of the slope twenty feet below them. There was no jarring impact, instead the branches bent under the weight and cushioned their fall. Before they had even stopped, Tarzan was already running along the boughs, his balance perfect even with Jane wrapped around his shoulders.

He vaulted into another tree further down the incline, occasionally using his arms to swing them across a gap or to ascend higher.

Utilizing this combination of running, leaping, and swinging he used the trees as stepping-stones until they reached the lofts of mighty trees lining the bank of the fast-flowing river that poured from the caldera lake. On these thick branches Tarzan easily hopped from one tree to another, sometimes descending into the heart of the trees—forcing Jane to duck as branches whipped her cheek and ear. Several times they crossed the river, keeping high and safe in the trees.

Tarzan continued for half an hour without slowing his pace. Jane might well have been as light as cotton, as he never had to stop to reposition her. This allowed Jane time to appreciate her position, when she wasn't ducking from whipping branches. The ground sped by at an alarming rate, and she could only marvel how much distance they had covered. She suspected Tarzan could cover a day's jungle trek in mere hours through the canopy.

Tarzan jumped again—and Jane's stomach dropped as they plummeted toward the earth. This time it looked as though Tarzan had misjudged his position within the trees. They were freefalling straight toward a smaller treetop—

Leaves cracked past them as the canopy took the brunt of the fall. Jane had a fleeting glimpse of a troop of red colobus monkeys shrieking as they dropped through. Tarzan's steely grip snagged a vine to arrest their fall, and they were suddenly swinging horizontally. The abrupt change of direction almost made Jane let go. They swung in a wide arc before Tarzan released the vine and gently dropped into a glade of stunning yellow flowers. Jane slid from his back, feeling a little dizzy, and watched hundreds of brightly colored butterflies take to the air all around them. It was a wondrous sight.

She looked at Tarzan in confusion. "Are we resting here?" He wasn't out of breath and wore a stoic expression despite the beauty around them. "I thought we were going to D'Arnot?"

"D'Arnot." He gestured across the glade.

"This place?" Jane sagged in disappointment that she wasn't being returned to her father. She sat down on a mound of dirt and clutched her head. "I don't feel too good. I thought D'Arnot was a town."

Tarzan frowned and pointed to the dirt she was sitting on. "D'Arnot."

Jane was ready to vent her frustration at the imbecile. She no longer cared how strong he was . . . then she noticed bony fingers poking from the dirt beneath her.

She sprang off the mound; her sharp movements displaced more earth and revealed a fragment of a human skull beneath.

It was D'Arnot.

•   •   •

"He came this way," said Mister David. He was hunched on the ground examining the remains of a campfire.

"You're certain it was him?" asked Archie.

Mister David gestured to the fire, the discarded energy-bar wrapper and the roughly hacked bushes around them. "An elephant would leave less mess."

"Anybody with him?"

Mister David shook his head. "Robbie followed the river, probably thinking Jane was taken that way. Or swept away."

Archie had been watching the river but didn't recognize a single turn or kink as they followed it. "And do you think she could have been swept away?" Archie tried to keep the tension from his voice; it was something that had been festering at the back of his mind since they had discovered no evidence of kidnappers.

Mister David considered this. "Yes. Nowhere for her to go ashore, so Robbie followed the river. I would do the same."

Clark stood on the banks of the river, studying the current. "Then we can make more time on the water. Get the raft out."

The raft would only take seven, so four of his men would have to return to Karibu Mji as they had to leave room if they found Robbie and Jane. Archie asked for two volunteers to continue searching. Anil, the logger from India, readily agreed; he had always enjoyed Robbie's company and was concerned. The other volunteer was Serge, a close friend of Mister David who shared his taste for adventure.

It took forty minutes to clear a path to the river and set the raft up on the shore. Provisions were refreshed from the four returning loggers, who stayed until the five men were pushed out on the raft.

The strong current gripped the light inflatable and the two oarsmen—Clark near the front and Serge at the back—struggled with the telescopic paddles to keep the boat straight. With the exception of Clark, no man was particularly adept at handling the craft, so they collided with several half-submerged logs—one of which Serge hit with his paddle in the mistaken belief it was a crocodile.

Their pace increased. With only the sound of splashing oars and the monkeys and birds around them, it would have been a pleasant excursion if not for the urgency that propelled them from one meandering bend to the next.

Mister David crouched at the prow, his keen eyes scanning the water and riverbank for and any signs of Robbie or Jane.

Half an hour passed before Mister David held up his hand.

"Stop!"

Clark looked around to see what the danger was. "Stop? How the hell can we stop? This thing doesn't have a brake!"

"Hippos!" hissed Mister David.

Now Clark could see them, like brown barrels just breaking the surface ahead. Beyond they could see where the three rivers became one and the water churned with powerful currents.

"They don't look dangerous," said Archie. He couldn't remember if they were or not. "I read on the Internet that they're fine in the water. Look at the bank. If Jane was in the water, this'd be the perfect place for her to get ashore."

Mister David gave him an incredulous look. "Of course they are dangerous!"

The hippos had picked up the scent of the group long before they saw them, and the moment their poor eyesight made out the yellow raft the alarm call went up. The bloat of hippos began loudly snorting and grunting, sounding like a herd of cattle. Then they submerged without leaving a ripple on the surface.

"What did I tell you?" said Archie. "Head to the bank, now!"

Clark and Serge delivered swift strokes toward the bank. Serge stabbed his paddle in again—and was surprised to hit something beneath the surface. The metal oar slipped from his grasp as a hippo rose beneath them in a flurry of whitewater.

The raft twisted sharply out of the water, tossing Archie, Mister David, and Serge out, then splashed back down. Clark, still aboard, was smashed flat on his face. Anil had gripped the boat's safety rope to secure his position, but was now looking into the hippo's gaping maw. The hippo's massive ivory canine teeth clashed down inches away from the petrified logger—puncturing the rubber with a loud hiss.

Mister David and Serge desperately swam for shore. Archie treaded water and watched helplessly as the hippo tore into the raft again. This time the flapping rubber caught on its tusk and, as the animal pulled, the raft half submerged. Anil jumped into the water and swam for the bank. Clark was still on board, his foot tangled in a rope, the deflating rubber folding around him as the hippo pulled him down.

"Clark!"

Archie swam as fast as he could to the stricken raft. He grabbed the side and reached in for Clark. Only Clark's thrashing feet were visible. The rest of him was trapped under water, smothered as the limp rubber slowly tangled around him. Archie fumbled for the knife strapped to Clark's exposed calf. The hippo had reached the bottom of the river, so only the tail of the raft was still on the surface—but now the animal powered forward along the riverbed, dragging the boat with it. Archie almost lost his grip as he was propelled sideways.

"Hold on, Clark!"

He unsheathed the knife and hacked at the rubber around Clark. Clark forced himself free as the rubber cocoon split open and Archie dragged him to the surface. Clark coughed up water and sucked in a lungful of air, his face bright red. He had been seconds away from drowning.

Archie pulled his friend to the bank. Slip-sliding through the mud, they collapsed ashore, helped by Mister David, Anil, and Serge, who had beaten them to safety. They watched as the remains of the raft, and all their provisions, sank beneath the muddy water.

Clark was still breathing hard. He looked at Archie, and then punched him in the arm. "Don't you ever believe the crap you read on the Internet!"

• • •

Jane was proud she hadn't screamed. She was no judge, but she thought the grave must have been there for several years. She looked at Tarzan, suddenly afraid. Had he killed the man?

Tarzan knelt down and covered the exposed bones with scoops of dirt. He didn't exhibit revulsion in his actions, but Jane thought she detected a trace of sadness.

"D'Arnot, Tarzan's friend."

"D-did you kill him?" Jane couldn't believe she'd spoken the question aloud, but she needed an answer.

If Tarzan was angered by the comment he didn't show it, he just shook his head. "D'Arnot friend, not enemy."

His answer calmed Jane a little.

"You want to see D'Arnot." He gestured to the mound.

"Did he arrive on the plane? The aircraft? Er," Jane tried to think of any way she could describe the airplane in simple terms.

Tarzan surprised her with his answer. "No. Airplane always been here. D'Arnot teached Tarzan to speak. He teached Tarzan about the world beyond."

"How did he die? Was it an animal?"

A dark look crossed Tarzan's face. "D'Arnot leave Tarzan. Tarzan find him dead."

Genuine regret flooded Tarzan's face and Jane felt guilty for accusing him of killing his friend. She automatically reached out an arm to comfort him, but hesitated. She wasn't sure how he'd react.

"Where'd he come from?"

"D'Arnot was French soldier from a place called," Tarzan hesitated as he recalled the name, "United Nations. Here to stop war, keep peace. D'Arnot killed for helping Tarzan."

Jane's mind was racing. Whoever D'Arnot was, he'd done an excellent job at teaching him English. "I'm sure he didn't die because he helped you." She tried to sound consoling, but it did little to break Tarzan's mood. "How long did you know him? How long was he here?"

Tarzan frowned, searching for his words. Jane assumed that it had been many years since he'd had the opportunity to speak English.

Jane decided to change tack.

"Where do you come from?" Tarzan pointed to the mountains. "No, I mean, where were you born? Who were your parents?" She knew she was asking too many questions, but she was relieved Tarzan was finally speaking and she needed answers.

"Mother was an ape, Kala. She dead too."

Jane giggled and shook her head. "No, seriously." Tarzan treated her to a stern look and she realized he was being serious. "Your mother can't be . . . that's impossible."

"Kala Tarzan's mother. She dead."

Jane remained silent. The grief on Tarzan's face was all too real. She had trouble believing that Tarzan was on board the plane when it crashed—how could he have survived in the wilderness since being a baby? That was surely impossible. Perhaps he had lost his memory and had invented his past?

"You've been on your own for a long time?"

"Not alone. With family." He smiled, but Jane saw something familiar in his eyes, something she had seen every day in the mirror. Loneliness. She had never before thought it would be possible to feel lonely surrounded by so many people, but her life in Karibu Mji had proved otherwise. Even with Robbie for company, she had never felt so alone. In many ways, she could see some of Robbie in Tarzan—the stubbornness and a past wreathed in mystery. Oddly, this thought made her feel at ease. Tarzan definitely was not the killer she'd first taken him for. He had cared for her, healed her, and the evident sorrow when he had spoken of D'Arnot convinced her he was telling the truth.

She suddenly felt weak, and the wound in her leg throbbed. She rubbed it, hissing at the pain.

"Rest," stated Tarzan.

"I need a doctor," said Jane as she sucked in a sharp breath. "You know, medicine man, healer . . . medic?"

"Tarzan heal you."

"I don't think Tarzan can heal me. No offence, but a Ph.D in tree roots and," she touched the sap on her scalp, "whatever this goop is, is not going to cure me. I need tablets, antibiotics. Medicine." She wasn't getting through to him. "I need to get back home."

"Too weak. When you strong again."

Jane *was* too weak to argue. She sat down, hoping the dizziness would pass. She noticed movement across the glade. For a moment she thought it was a trick of the light . . . was it a man, maybe her father? That was wishful thinking. She rubbed her eyes and looked again. It was a huge silverback gorilla but she wasn't alarmed, she felt safe in Tarzan's company.

"Your family have come to find you," teased Jane.

Tarzan's face was set in a snarl. His eyes never left the silverback as more gorillas, blackbacks and females, sauntered into the glade, picking at the flowers. The silverback galloped toward Tarzan, pounding its chest. Then stopped and stood sideways, displaying its mighty bulk as its knuckles pawed the earth. It grunted a challenge at Tarzan.

"Terkoz not family. Terkoz enemy," snarled Tarzan.

Jane suddenly felt alarmed. She couldn't tell one silverback from the next and was sitting between the menacing gorilla and Tarzan.

Terkoz's eyes fixed on her. His face was covered in scars from previous battles for dominance, and this was one fight the ape refused to back down from.

With a bellow of rage, Terkoz charged.

9

Robbie couldn't stop scratching the bites on his neck and the welts on his fingers. At least the pain was a distraction from his concern over Jane and the fate of the camp.

The rebel guerrillas chose their path with care but their progress was swift as they used animal trails rather than hack through the thick bush. Robbie kept behind, always out of sight. The noise of the six men made following them easy. A few times Bapoto fell back and Robbie had almost blundered into him before darting into the greenery. During those times Bapoto's keen eyes scanned the trees for half a minute, before joining his men.

The more Robbie saw Bapoto, the more he was reminded of his stepfather. They had the same cruel eyes, the same powerful build and, Robbie was certain, the same ruthlessness.

With each tiring step, Robbie's mind drifted back to New York.

Skipping school to work in a garage allowed him to find happiness. He learned to drive and lost himself in the intricate mechanics of engines. The garage was a whole new world and a place he felt so safe that he would often sleep there for days on end . . .

Robbie stumbled on a rotting log. No, he refused to think about the past. Jane was more important. He couldn't change the past but he could help Jane and his new friends.

The memories continued to flow unbidden.

Climbing the creaking stairs after being away for almost a week of freedom. His hand ran across the peeling wallpaper. The smell of nicotine and alcohol; a single naked light bulb in the hall. Robbie's memory threw these small details into sharp relief.

I don't want to remember, Robbie said to himself. He looked around the jungle, eager for something to distract him.

His mother's bedroom door was ajar and he caught a glimpse of her snoring on the bed, half a dozen empty wine bottles on the dresser.

I hate you, thought Robbie. He slapped a fly that was crawling on his neck, but the stinging pain didn't vanquish the memories. He fought against them, but they broke into his consciousness like a tidal wave of regret.

Laughter from the television in the living room. His stepfather was home. His stepfather, the source of all his anger and hatred, which he focused on the filthy overweight . . .

His memories clumsily cycled through his head like a film with frames missing.

He entered Sophie's room. There was still a small Mexican hat nailed to it; a cherished gift from some long-lost uncle.

He wanted to tell her all about the escape plan he had conjured up while in the garage. A plan guaranteed to get them both to a better place.

She was under the sheets, unmoving.

No!

A stale smell in the air.

"NO!" Robbie growled to the jungle. He stopped on the muddy animal track and put his head in his hands as he recalled the events with sickening clarity.

He nudged her. Whispered her name, but she didn't respond.

With rising panic he shook her thin frame, noticing fresh purple bruises on her arm. Her pale face limply rolled to once side, a nasty lump on the side of her forehead where she'd been struck the week before had now gone bad.

Why hadn't he had the guts to face his stepfather then?

The faint click-clack of steel in the real world made him freeze. He listened intently as the rebels primed their weaponry in readiness for an imminent attack. Robbie couldn't see them, but maybe Bapoto had finally spotted him and was laying an ambush?

Robbie slowly edged from the trail and pushed his way through the tall bamboo that towered around him, its leaves casting everything in a green hue. He trod as stealthily as possibly, but still couldn't avoid crunching detritus underfoot. Judging from the direction of the rebels' whispered conversations, he was arcing around them, inching slowly ahead.

The bamboo thinned out, revealing a natural ridge a couple of feet higher than the riverbank below—where Archie, Clark, and Mister David were having a heated argument with Anil and Serge.

Robbie couldn't believe his luck. They had circled back to the same spot on the river.

However, before he could warn his friends of the ambush a volley of automatic gunfire cracked through the jungle and Bapoto appeared above them, menacingly waving his AK-47 rifle.

• • •

Tarzan and Terkoz collided with a terrible thud of flesh. Tarzan was unable to compete with Tarkoz's weight, but his dexterity made all the difference. He acrobatically flipped over the gorilla, hooking his arm around Terkoz's bull-neck and squeezing him in a chokehold.

Jane was flat on the ground, scrambling for safety, but she didn't get very far before one of the blackbacks stepped in her way. Jane sucked in her breath, bracing for an attack. Instead the gorilla's intelligent eyes swept across her, deducing she was not a threat. Then it sat down next to her and watched the fight, making no attempt to get involved. Sensing she was safe for the moment, Jane watched too.

Terkoz tried to shake Tarzan free, but to no avail. The chokehold was too firm and Terkoz struggled to breathe. Tarzan's teeth sunk into the lank fur, biting into the flesh, his nails scratching like talons. Terkoz roared and suddenly folded to the ground, bringing

Tarzan with him. It was a cunning move. The ape rolled, intending to crush Tarzan—but the human sprang nimbly aside.

Crouching low, Tarzan circled the beast. An inhuman guttural snarl issued from Tarzan's bloodied lips. Terkoz looked unsteady on his feet; Tarzan's bites and gouges were having an effect.

Jane was mesmerized by the struggle as the combatants circled. Tarzan's hand went for the dagger on his hip, but he hesitated to unsheathe it. That would be an unfair fight.

Terkoz swung a chunky fist—which Tarzan easily ducked. Another blow was evaded and the ape was becoming frustrated as they circled again. Terkoz suddenly rushed Tarzan, catching him unprepared.

Jagged teeth bit into Tarzan's arm. He snarled and rolled aside, springing lithely to his feet. Blood spurted from the wound, but Tarzan didn't give it anything more than a cursory glance. He appeared to be enjoying the fight.

Terkoz charged again and Tarzan fell on his back. Jane shrieked in fear as the silverback bore down on him.

But Tarzan had a plan. His feet kicked into Terkoz's stomach as his hand tugged the ape's arm, forcing the brute off-balance. Tarzan used the leverage to toss the heavy gorilla over him and the goliath crashed headfirst into the earth. Tarzan used a handspring to flip to his feet, then delivered a powerful kick to the animal's flank, thrusting Terkoz on his back.

Jane was taken aback by the combination of skill and savage strength used in the fight. She watched as Tarzan uncoiled the rope from his belt and formed a noose. Tarzan circled victoriously around Terkoz and swung the noose menacingly.

The brute was down, but refused to submit. Tarzan cockily approached and Terkoz sat up and made a swing for him—

Tarzan had expected the jab and looped the noose around Terkoz's forearm, then somersaulted over the confused gorilla. Before Terkoz could turn to follow, Tarzan tugged the rope with all his might and Terkoz's fist slammed into his own face, forcing him to collapse in a complete daze.

The other gorillas in the glade knew the fight was over and hooted their approval. Tarzan shook the rope free and placed one foot on

Terkoz's chest in an undeniable act of victory. The silverback snarled, but was too beaten to stop him. Tarzan raised his head to the sky and roared.

The hairs on the back of Jane's neck stood up; the gorillas around her lapsed into silence and birds in the surrounding trees took flight.

Satisfied that all in the band accepted his dominance, Tarzan crossed to Jane and helped her stand. She was shaking, partly from the fight but mostly because Tarzan now looked every bit the killer. Terkoz's blood stained Tarzan's mouth and cheeks, and his own wound was freely bleeding. But his eyes twinkled with life. The fight had not fazed him in the least. The nearest blackback kept its distance from Tarzan, and coughed to acknowledge they had no quarrel.

"You almost killed a gorilla!" Jane exclaimed. "With your bare hands!"

Tarzan shook his head. He looked offended. "Tarzan not kill Terkoz."

Jane glanced at the big silverback. He sat upright, swaying slightly. A female crossed to him and gently touched the wounds on his head.

"But Tarzan won." He looked at Jane with concern. "You need rest."

Jane pointed to his wound and winced. A flap of skin hung open, revealing the raw flesh beneath. "You need stitches on that."

Tarzan glanced at the wound with indifference. He led Jane from the glade, the band of gorillas parting from their path. Once again, Tarzan had proved who ruled the jungle.

• • •

Archie hunkered down as the shots rang out. His first thought was that Serge, who carried a gun, was using it to force them into going back to Karibu Mji as he been insisting on doing, instead of trampling through the jungle without any supplies.

Then Archie saw Bapoto stride from the bamboo, the AK-47 jauntily angled on his hip. The two men instantly recognized one another. Tafari's right-hand man usually did the dirty work.

"Bapoto, it's me, Archie Porter." Archie stood, keeping his hands up.

Bapoto laughed in surprise. "Just the man I was looking for, *ami*. How God smiles on me to bring us together in this hellhole."

Rain began to patter around them and Bapoto gestured to the sky as if it emphasized his point.

"You were looking for us?" That was a disturbing thought. Of course, that must mean they had Jane. "I want my daughter back."

Bapoto's confident smile vanished. "Daughter?"

Archie had been careful not to divulge too much about life at their camp. He had always known it was dangerous to mention he had brought his family. "The girl you took is my daughter. She's done nothing wrong."

Other rebels emerged from the trees, their weapons aimed at Archie's group. Bapoto slid down the ravine and approached them.

"I don't know what you're talking about, but I can guess why you're here, eh? Planning another attack on our barracks?" He threw the rifle over his shoulder and drew his beloved kukri from his belt. The blade was stained from numerous battles and he found it far more intimidating than a gun.

It was Archie's turn to be puzzled, his eyes darting to the blade. "I don't know what you're talking about."

"Oh, course not," Bapoto sneered, idly waving the knife. "Why else would you be out here? Tafari sent me to give you a little message. On your knees."

Archie hesitated. "My daughter's missing—"

Bapoto suddenly kicked Archie's legs from under him. Archie landed on his back, hard enough to wind him.

"That's better," cooed Bapoto menacingly. He circled Archie, keeping one eye on the other loggers. "You damaged our vehicles and cut our power. Tafari wants to know why you would do this. He wants to know who you are working for."

From the trees Robbie watched with a growing sense of panic. It was obvious that a third party was causing the trouble, but it looked like Bapoto was determined to shed blood over it. What could he do against seven armed men?

"There's been some mistake," said Archie. He kept his voice calm and reasonable, but inside he was terrified. "We thought you had attacked us and kidnapped my daughter. That's why we came to find you. I want my daughter back right now!"

Bapoto wasn't listening; he was enjoying his power trip too much. He swished the knife menacingly. "What will it be? A hand? Leg? Or maybe one of your men?" He pointed his rifle at Anil. "I don't care which."

"There's been a mistake!"

"And you made it." He gently rested the sharp blade under Archie's chin. "Now decide."

Anil leapt to his feet and tried to make a run for it.

BAM! A gunshot rang out and Anil fell to the ground, blood smattering his back.

Everybody looked around in shock. Oudry had fired; his rifle was still pointed at the dead man. Bapoto laughed heartily as he looked at the terror on Archie's face.

A metallic click suddenly echoed across the ravine, and Oudry felt cold steel pressed against his temple.

"Drop the guns," yelled Robbie.

Bapoto spun around in surprise as Robbie appeared from the bamboo. His disheveled appearance was perfect camouflage in the jungle. He held his revolver firmly against the rebel's head. He just hoped nobody could see how much he was shaking.

Archie used the distraction to snatch the AK-47 from Bapoto's shoulder and jabbed it in his ribs.

"The knife," prompted Archie.

Bapoto didn't drop the blade, instead he slid it back in his belt. With a snarl, Archie cracked him across the back of the head with the rifle's stock and Bapoto dropped to his knees.

"You're surrounded," yelled Robbie. "We've been following you for some time." He was running on adrenalin and had no idea if his ploy would work. "Throw your weapons down."

Bapoto scowled. His own paranoia was enough to convince him Robbie was telling the truth. "Do as he says!" he commanded his men.

Oudry was the first to drop his gun, then the other rebels reluctantly followed and raised their hands. That was the cue for Clark, Mister David, and Serge to retrieve the weapons and hold the rebels at gunpoint. Robbie jumped down the ravine to join Clark.

"You OK?" hissed Clark.

"Fine."

Archie prodded Bapoto with the gun barrel. "Up. Now I have no idea what you imagine we've done, but we're not your enemies."

Robbie spoke up. "They don't have Jane."

Archie looked quizzically at him. "Where is she?"

"I don't know. But they don't have her."

Archie blinked in surprise. He didn't know what to say. If the rebels didn't have her then she must be lost. His heart sank. That meant finding her would be almost impossible especially after wasting over twenty-four hours on this wild goose chase.

Clark spoke up and nudged Bapoto. "You boys better scram before someone gets an itchy trigger finger and seeks revenge for our friend there." He nodded toward Anil.

The rebels slowly retreated into the jungle, keeping their hands in clear view. Bapoto stared malevolently at Archie.

"I'll see you soon," he muttered. "*J'aurai ta peau!*"

"We're not your enemy," Archie said. "Somebody attacked our camp too and took my daughter."

Bapoto made it to the edge of the bamboo and lowered his hands, his snake-like gaze on Archie. "Today you made a powerful enemy."

Archie felt a chill down his spine.When they'd gone, Mister David rushed to check on Anil. He was clearly dead.

"We must bury him here," he said softly. "We can't take him back."

Robbie looked at Anil and felt a deep sadness. They'd shared many jokes around the campfire and now Anil was dead because of his impulsive desire to look for Jane.

Archie laid a hand on Robbie's shoulder. "That was a brave thing you did, Robert."

Robbie held up the gun and flipped open the cylinders. They were empty.

"No bullets."

"Then you're even braver. Any coward can carry a gun."

"And any fool can go hurtlin' through the bush on his own and almost get himself killed!" said Clark. Now that Robbie had been found, his relief had transformed into anger. "Anil would still be alive if we hadn't come tearin' through here lookin' for you!"

"I did it because nobody was looking for Jane!" Robbie wasn't about to be used as a scapegoat, even if Clark was echoing his own thoughts.

"We had a plan! You shouldn't have bucked off like that!"

"We would have probably come this way anyway, and Anil would still have been killed," said Archie calmly. Clark spluttered, not expecting his mate to back Robbie up. "And we could have all been shot if it wasn't for Robbie."

Clark snatched the pistol from Robbie but didn't say a word. Robbie couldn't take his eyes off the dead man.

Archie recognized the guilt on Robbie face and felt sorry for him. "What did you find out about Jane?"

"Just what Bapoto said. They have had attacks on their base, just like us. They were looking for you because they thought you were responsible. Not because they took Jane."

"So she really is lost." Archie was silent for a moment as the darkest thoughts crept into his imagination. Then, the words that he had dared think but had feared to say out loud tumbled from his lips: "C-could she be . . . dead?"

Robbie knew that couldn't be true. Fate couldn't be so cruel.

"No, she's not. She isn't lost. She's with whoever attacked both camps. Find them and we find Jane."

Robbie watched as a glimmer of hope lit Archie's face. Nothing further needed to be said. It was time they dug a shallow grave for their fallen comrade.

• • •

Jane thought she was dying. She recalled walking from the glade, then her legs gave way and she spiraled into a never-ending pit of darkness . . . only to wake up back in the aircraft fuselage. The rain clouds had blown away, revealing a vivid blue sky. Birds flittered in the twisted roots and creepers that clung to the aircraft, the occasional frond poking through a smashed window.

She sat upright—and immediately provoked a hoot from Tana, who had been watching over her. Karnath had lain against Jane's side, keeping her warm, and now he hooted with excitement. Tarzan came running in moments later, holding a large fruit husk that contained water. He put it to her lips.

"Drink."

Jane drank the water, grimacing at its odd taste. Tarzan followed it up with a piece of thin bark.

"Eat."

"This? It's a piece of a tree." She examined the bark closely; it had an acrid smell and inside was sticky sap. "I can't eat that."

Tarzan thrust the bark into her mouth and then covered it with his hand so she couldn't spit it out. "Eat!"

Jane felt the familiar tremble of fear. Tarzan could switch between gentle and fierce as quickly as the wind. She chewed the bark and found it had a sour taste but wasn't unpleasant. When she swallowed, Tarzan removed his hand, looking satisfied.

"What was that?"

"Medicine."

"I need real medicine. I need to go home." She noticed that her leg wound had been cleaned again even though the bite in Tarzan's shoulder was still untreated. He had elected to help her before himself. Once again, Jane's opinion of Tarzan seesawed as fast as his temper. "You're still hurt."

Tarzan poked his wound but he didn't react. Instead he reached for a pile of small nuts and a tin stowed at the back of the aircraft. The tin looked old and sported the word "biscuits" in a swirling faded font. Tarzan sat next to Jane and opened it.

Army ants swarmed around inside. They were all large-headed soldiers, the biggest specimens Jane had ever seen. Tarzan selected one and slammed the lid back down. With two fingers he pinched his wound together and with the other he carefully pushed the ant's oversized head across the seam. Tarzan quickly twisted the body to snap the head off, leaving part of the wound sutured with the dead ant's jaws. Jane watched in fascination as Tarzan repeated the action a dozen times until the wound was fully closed, then he took a small nut and squeezed it hard, and an oily residue dripped into the wound. Task complete, Tarzan flexed his arm and looked happy with the results. Jane studied the tiny heads holding the wound closed. They looked like little beads . . .

She inspected her wounded leg with a growing sense of revulsion as she realized that what she had assumed were bead-like stitches were in fact ants' heads! She fought the temptation to brush them off her leg, for no matter how disgusting, they bound the wound tightly together.

"Where did you learn to do all this?"

"My family know what good to eat." He pointed to Tana, now sitting in the doorway paying them no attention. "And D'Arnot know everything else."

Jane knew she was in no state to go anywhere, so she decided to get some answers from Tarzan. "Did D'Arnot find you here?"

"Tarzan save him from Sabor."

Jane sighed. This wasn't going to be easy. She stood up. Already her head felt clearer after consuming the concoction Tarzan had given her.

"Sabor? What is that?"

Tarzan treated her to an odd look, the kind of look Jane would give if she had to explain something very complex to an idiot.

"Sabor do this." He tapped her leg.

"Oh, a lion? OK. You saved him from a li— Sabor. And brought him here?"

"Tarzan heal D'Arnot. D'Arnot stay, teach Tarzan to speak. Teach the way of your world."

"You've never been outside the jungle?"

"D'Arnot want to take Tarzan to place called city, to meet other people." A look of sadness crossed his face.

"Have you never seen people before? Before D'Arnot, before me?"

Tarzan snarled. "Yes! People come to Tarzan's land. Kill it. Burn it. They evil people! Tarzan kill them!"

The aggression in his voice startled Jane as she once again ran through a gamut of feelings from sympathy to fear. She sat on a seat, the metal frame creaking under her weight. She looked Tarzan in the eye and remembered something her mother had once told her—never show fear to a dog because that's when it will bite. Jane had no desire for Tarzan to bite her.

"Killing them is . . . that's evil too." Tarzan clearly didn't understand. She looked around for inspiration, something that would help her explain the basic principles of good versus evil . . . then she saw something familiar cast aside on the floor. Several large pen-shaped fuel injectors—exactly like the ones ripped from the camp's bulldozer! She held them aloft as evidence.

"These are from our camp! You did this?" Tarzan shrugged, a smile playing on his lips, which widened the more irate Jane became. "You sabotaged us! Why would you do such a thing? Wait . . ." A worse thought occurred to her. "Tell me you didn't . . . you started the fire too, didn't you? The night I got lost and ended up here—you did that, didn't you?"

"Tarzan hate fire!"

"So it wasn't you?"

Tarzan smiled proudly. Lying wasn't a skill he needed. "It was . . . accident."

"AAARGH!" Jane threw the fuel injectors at Tarzan.

"You put me through this! You! How could you make my life more miserable?" Tears rolled down her cheeks. Tarzan curiously reached out to touch them but Jane batted his hand aside. "Don't touch me! Why did you do that? We didn't do you any harm!"

"People at camps kill Tarzan's land. They are evil."

It was a softly spoken statement and it derailed Jane's tantrum. For a moment, nothing but the birdsong outside and a few gentle grunts could be heard.

"We're not evil. We're just trying to make a living." Jane sat down on another seat, overwhelmed by the need to defend her father. "My mother ran away. Left my dad . . . and me. Took everything we had. Then Dad found out she owed a lot of money. We lost the house. And still my mom . . . didn't care." Jane stared at the floor, remembering how betrayed she'd felt. At the time she hadn't even considered her father must have felt the same. She'd never considered that at all, until now. Now she couldn't tell him.

"He had to quit his job. No matter what he made, it was never enough. And my mom owed money to a lot of bad people. Loan sharks. We couldn't pay them back so they set my dad up and he lost his medical license and was accused of things that ruined his reputation. We had to leave, hide. Then Archie hit on this stupid idea. It was illegal . . . but it wasn't in our country, right? I mean it's not like we're breaking any *real* laws. And the trees grow back. No harm done. We make enough money to start a better life someplace else. Start again."

She looked at Tarzan, expecting to see sympathy on his face, the same as Robbie had expressed when she'd bled her heart to him. Instead, Tarzan was angry.

"No harm?" His fists clenched. "No trees, no food. No shelter. No home. Animals killed because of evil people. Men with guns kill, not for food, for laughter. For nothing! They kill animal, they kill other men. They all bad!"

"You can't judge *us* like that! And we didn't kill anybody! You're getting us confused with those soldiers. The rebels are the ones killing people, not us!"

"Men all the same!" snapped Tarzan. The veins on his neck bulged as he contained his rage. "Tarzan fair. Send warnings for you to go."

"You moved the tree we cut down, didn't you?"

"Tarzan and Tantor take tree, hope people go. They do not."

Jane filed away the name Tantor for a later date. Right now she had to teach Tarzan the difference between right and wrong before he attempted to kill anybody. If he hadn't already. That thought was chilling.

"Not everybody is evil. We cut down the trees because . . . because we have to." She knew it was a really weak excuse, after all she had been shouting at her father for saying exactly the same thing. "You didn't kill that gorilla, Terkoz. Why?"

"Terkoz not evil. He not try kill Tarzan. He fight to be king. Not to kill for no reason."

Jane didn't have a response to that. In a twisted way it made sense. "So now you're king?"

"Tarzan king of jungle," he said with a sense of pride.

Jane smiled. That must have been something D'Arnot had told him. "So you're king of all the animals?"

"Yes."

She couldn't help but laugh. He must be delusional. "OK. If that's what you think . . . good. And you can speak to them too, I bet."

"Yes."

At the sound of her laughter Tarzan's anger disappeared, his mood as changeable as ever. Then, without a further word, he walked out.

Jane didn't know what to do. A normal argument over life and death shouldn't have ended so suddenly and without resolution. She followed him.

Tarzan sat cross-legged on the wing of the plane that extended over the cliff. He was gazing at the sun as it touched the mountain ridge. Jane preferred terra firma and sat on the roots of a huge tree and watched brightly colored birds flitting around her and the great apes slowly climbing back up the trail to settle for another night.

She had to make Tarzan understand they were not evil people and didn't deserve to be on the receiving end of his wrath. She decided the only way she could explain her point of view was by getting to know more about the strange young man.

10

Robbie was lost in his own world as the search party retraced their steps back to Karibu Mji. Bypassing the hippos and fording the river beneath the setting sun provided a terrifying challenge that ultimately passed without trouble.

As night crept in, Mister David created torches for everyone, lit with the trusty waterproof lighter he kept in a pocket. With the flaming torches they were able to follow Robbie's trail back to Karibu Mji. Muscles hurt and complaints were voiced as Mister David relentlessly drove them forward, only occasionally stopping for a few minutes' rest. Listening nervously to every sound around them as they walked, they were braced for an imminent attack from wild animals or, worse, the rebels. The weapons they had taken from Bapoto's men did little to reassure them.

Robbie had tried to raise the issue of who Jane's abductors could be now Tafari had been ruled out. But Mister David whispered his theories of evil forest spirits who came to abduct or kill local villagers and the conversation died. Nobody wanted to think about spirits in the depths of night, especially not Robbie, who was continually plagued by spirits of his past.

He had wanted nothing more than to climb from his impoverished home life and to build something better for him and his sister. He had tried to attend lessons in school, but his love for engines and machinery drew him toward garages. It was there he learned his skills until his Saturday job bled into the school week and it became an unofficial job. It was the only place he'd ever received praise. His Chinese manager encouraged him to expand his skills by working on every new vehicle that entered the shop, from the lowliest car to the most complex truck.

He and Sophie had whispered about what they would do when he'd saved enough to move out of home. It was a dream that helped them cope with their stepfather's violence. Robbie had thrown every spare second he had into the job in order to save more money, even sleeping in the garage whenever he could. But that meant spending less time watching over Sophie.

And that had been a terrible mistake.

If only he had paid more attention. If only he had acted quicker.

It was months later that Clark had taught him not to labor over past mistakes but to learn from them and move on. But Clark wasn't aware of the full picture . . .

Robbie tried to ignore his thoughts and looked at the faces of the exhausted men around him. Anil was missing. The image of his brutally murdered body struck a chord with Robbie.

Sophie's dead.

Robbie spent several nights curled under trees in Central Park. When the cold started to bite he found back alleys warmed by ventilation grids over the subway below. Stealing food from shops had been easy enough, and he had been able to lose himself in the streets when he had been caught.

However, as each day passed he felt the net closing in on him. Police cars would appear with greater frequency. That could only mean they were looking for him.

They knew what he had done.

He left New York, crossing the river to New Jersey. From there he watched the colossal container ships heading out to unknown exotic locations. This was his chance to escape.

For several nights he hid amongst the industrial containers at Port

Jersey. Then he saw his chance and stowed away aboard a freighter. Robbie had no idea where he was heading and in his grief-stricken rage he didn't care.

He sloshed through a puddle, bringing him sharply back to the present. The wet hems of his jeans rubbed uncomfortably against his skin. He lowered his flashlight so he could roll them up. As he revealed his shin he saw it was covered in leeches, swelling as he watched them suck his blood.

This was going to be a long night.

• • •

A cacophony of angry rapid coughs woke Jane from a deep slumber. She was instantly alert. Any signs of her dizziness had vanished thanks to the herbal remedies Tarzan had forced down her. She crossed to the opening of the plane and peered into the darkness.

The gorillas were agitated. Kerchak galloped across the plateau beating his chest and shaking the branches of every tree he passed. The blackbacks barked at some unknown danger and tore clumps of earth from the ground in a threatening display of power. In the trees, monkeys added to the furor.

Tarzan suddenly appeared from the darkness behind Jane. He looked tense, peering into the jungle for any signs of movement.

"What's happening?" whispered Jane.

"*Manu* see enemy." He pointed toward the monkeys, and Jane filed away Tarzan's word for them.

The clamor intensified and Tarzan crept toward the aircraft's tail, crouching under its tail stabilizers. Jane followed close behind him.

There was a sudden burst of activity and with a terrifying roar, something leapt out of the trees, knocking Kerchak backward. In the light of the full moon Jane saw a lioness rake her claws across the silverback. She recognized the big cat immediately from the tear in its ear—it was the creature Tarzan fought when he first saved her. It must be Sabor!

The lioness landed in the throng of apes and roared again. Females clutched their young and ran for cover as two blackbacks charged Sabor. One was met with a slash from Sabor's talons that tore into his arm.

Jane was astonished that Sabor had tracked her up the mountain. She knew from Esmée that lions seldom entered the jungle this high up, favoring the lowland forest and grassy plains. However, intensive farming was shrinking their preferred hunting ground and forcing them to hunt wider. She saw Tana and Karnath running away from the fight and was glad the vulnerable younger gorillas had been shepherded to safety.

But she soon realized that that was Sabor's plan. The wily cat was not alone.

Two more lionesses sprang from their cover across the plateau to the exact spot where Sabor had driven the female gorillas.

Jane watched in shock as a lioness clamped her slavering jaws around Tana's arm. With a shriek, Tana dropped Karnath and fought the feline. Karnath was batted aside by a huge paw as the other big cats circled their injured prey, tails pointed, ready for the kill.

"NO!"

Jane's voice echoed across the plateau. Tarzan had already vaulted the tail wing to pursue Sabor, but altered course when he heard Jane's warning. He sprinted across the clearing to help Tana, and Jane realized that he was about to fight the lionesses with his bare hands.

One cat bit hard into Tana's leg, pinning her down. The ape swung blindly about, clobbering the other cat and dazing it. The lioness with her teeth in the gorilla suddenly felt her back legs yanked way, as Tarzan gripped the underside of her belly with one muscular arm and punched her in the throat with the other. The lioness immediately released Tana, finding she suddenly had to fight for her own life.

The lioness Tana had sent flying recovered and pounced at Tarzan, wicked claws glinting in the moonlight—but she didn't make it. Kerchak slammed into the cat and both were sent flying into the side of the aircraft.

Jane cowered behind the plane's tail and watched the struggle. There was a glint of steel as Tarzan drew his knife and slashed the big cat across the flank. It was a vicious wound but fair retaliation for the fours claw marks that raked his back. Tarzan circled the lioness, who hunched, poised to spring. Farther away Kerchak was swinging powerful blows into his yowling opponent.

Then Jane saw movement. A small body was crawling back to its injured mother—Karnath! The young ape was oblivious to the danger he was edging toward.

Without thinking, Jane ran from cover—stumbling on a section of the aircraft's broken stabilizer hidden under the grass—and scooped Karnath into her arms. She felt the fluffy damp fur press against her face, and could hear the youngster's heart pounding in fear. Karnath hooked his long arms around Jane as she cradled him.

Tarzan swung the knife again, but his opponent deftly avoided the blade and went for his arm. With lightning reflexes, Tarzan gripped the cat's powerful jaw with his free hand, pulling it back before she could sever his limb. But then he lost his balance and the lioness pinned him down.

Jane felt helpless. Maybe there was something she could use as a weapon? She turned—and froze.

Sabor crouched in Jane's path, recognizing the scent of the prey she had been hunting.

The cat was only half her height, but outrunning her would be impossible. Jane's fear suddenly evaporated. Her mind felt sharper than ever as she assessed the situation. Every sound was amplified; every movement obvious. The muscles in Sabor's hindquarters twitched with anticipation and Jane knew the beast was about to pounce. Through her bare feet, Jane could feel every stone and blade of grass . . . and something else.

With reflexes she never knew she possessed, Jane dropped to her knees and tore the shattered aluminium tail stabiliser from the ground. With Karnath still hanging from her neck, she swung the wing fragment at the leaping cat with as much force as she could muster.

The metal panel buckled as it struck Sabor across the head. The cat soared over Jane and landed awkwardly on her side. Jane didn't look back at her handiwork as she bolted for the safety of the plane.

Tarzan used both feet to kick the lioness from him. The big cat was catapulted into a tree trunk with bone-breaking force. Tarzan was on his feet in an instant. With one sweep of the battlefield he processed the multiple threats: The lioness had recovered from striking the tree but was now limping as she ran toward him with a snarl; Kerchak's foe had escaped him and was also bearing down on Tarzan.

The third lioness, Sabor, was stalking Jane.

Jane held Karnath tightly as she ran for the aircraft. She heard Tarzan give an extraordinary warbling cry before two lions pounced on him simultaneously.

The warble was answered by a fierce roar from every gorilla in a unified battle cry. And then a new voice answered from the jungle—the unmistakable sound of another wild cat.

As Jane ducked into her refuge, she began to wonder if Tarzan could really speak with the animals. She unhooked Karnath from her neck and gently placed him at the back of the plane. Then she looked around for anything she could use to block the way in, but the gap was too big.

A paw suddenly shattered a window and swatted her. Sabor's claws grazed her scalp but failed to draw blood. Jane screamed and rolled aside. Karnath shrieked with alarm as Sabor's silhouette blocked the entrance, and gave a throaty growl of victory.

Tarzan had known pain all his life. The stabbing of claws into his leg and arms would have stopped anybody else, but for Tarzan, the lioness that had latched on to him was simply a means to an end. It enabled him to keep a grip on the beast as he twisted around—and used her body as a weapon to bat the second cat aside.

Both animals howled in anger. The swatted lioness skittered across the plateau and a mob of angry gorillas descended on her in unified force. With a yowl of defeat, the cat sprinted for the trees as powerful fists hammered her.

Tarzan pushed the remaining cat off him. She wasn't going to give in without a fight now she had tasted his blood. Tarzan glanced over at the plane—Sabor was stepping inside! Then he caught a glimpse of a sleek shadow leaping from the trees in her pursuit.

He turned back to his immediate foe—too late. The lioness was already airborne. He went for his knife but it clattered to the ground out of his reach as she slammed into him. They both tumbled dangerously close the edge of the plateau.

• • •

Jane picked up a thin branch from her bed and swished it at Sabor. The slender limb whipped across the feline's snout and forced her to hesitate.

Sabor roared. The cat's breath was rank. Karnath screeched and clambered for safety into a broken overhead luggage compartment.

Jane used the only weapon she had left. She stamped her foot and yelled as loud as she could.

Unbelievably, Sabor was dragged backward through the entrance. Any notion Jane had that she was the cause was extinguished when she saw a lithe black shape straddling Sabor's back. It had pulled the lioness out of the plane and was wrestling her to the ground. Jane raced toward the door for a better view.

A slightly smaller black cat sank its jaws into Sabor's back, pinning the lioness to the floor. It was a leopard, but rather than the yellowish fur and distinctive clusters of black rosettes Jane had seen on other leopards, this panther was different. Moonlight reflected from powerful muscles flexing under fur as black as midnight. It had scored a powerful blow against Sabor. Blood discolored the back of the lioness's neck.

Sabor shucked the leopard off and swiped both forepaws in a desperate bid to strike back. Although smaller than Sabor, the panther was much more agile. It pounced on the side of the aircraft, claws attaching it to the covering undergrowth, from where it cuffed Sabor across the muzzle.

Sabor retreated from the panther and saw that Jane had inadvertently exposed herself as a fresh target. Before Jane could move, the panther leapt between her and Sabor as if it were protecting her.

The panther gave a raspy bellow and Sabor retreated. The lioness looked around for the support of her hunting pride but saw only the enraged gorillas trampling toward her, and her remaining sister wrestling Tarzan on the edge of the cliff. With a defiant roar, she fled into the jungle. Some of the apes gave a half-hearted pursuit, throwing rocks and branches at her. The panther snorted at Jane, then turned its attention to Tarzan.

• • •

Tarzan wrestled the lioness to the floor. The big cat used its weight to roll on top of him—but didn't stop. Focused only on the life-or-death fight, the lioness continued rolling straight off the edge of the precipice, pulling Tarzan with her. Tarzan's fingers raked mud and grass as he was hauled over the edge.

"TARZAN!" Jane began running—but there was no way she could reach him in time.

Tarzan plummeted.

"NO!"

Tarzan and the lioness fell seven feet until they slammed into a rocky ledge that dislodged the grip the beast had on him. The ledge crumbled from the impact and they dropped again—but Tarzan's hand was already moving to his waist . . .

Jane stopped in her tracks as a vine lasso shot over the rim of the plateau and caught on a broken tree limb. The rope pulled taut and she ran to the cliff edge as Tarzan heaved himself up, back to safety. He was breathing hard and was covered in blood from multiple wounds, but he was smiling as he stood—then he bellowed triumphantly.

Jane ran to Tarzan's aid but didn't get too close because the panther was rubbing itself against his leg and purring. Tarzan scratched the cat between the ears.

"Good Sheeta."

Jane surprised herself by hesitantly extending her hand to the panther, but had second thoughts when Sheeta turned to her. Tarzan gave her an encouraging nod and Jane gently stroked Sheeta's velvet fur.

"Thank you, Sheeta," she whispered.

The cat purred louder, then set about cleaning itself. Jane examined Tarzan's wounds, but his attention lay over her shoulder. She turned to see the gorillas were circling something. She followed Tarzan, her fear of the apes dispelled as she pushed through their ranks.

Tana lay at the center. The lions had inflicted terrible wounds and caused her to lose a lot of blood. It was clear from a single glance that Tana's wounds were beyond Tarzan's healing. Her breaths came in shallow rasps and she feebly laid a hand on Karnath, who sat on her chest. The little ape's eyes were wide. He didn't understand why his mother wouldn't stand.

Tears stung Jane's eyes and she was flooded with intense sorrow. The gentle ape had taken it upon herself to watch over Jane. Now she lay dying because she had protected her only child.

Tana gave a soft grumble, as if to assure Karnath that everything would be all right. Jane felt a soft leathery hand suddenly press against hers and she looked into Tana's brown eyes only to see the life drain out of them.

Karnath cried in alarm as his mother's chest grew still.

Tarzan bowed his head in silent grief at the loss of another of his family. Kerchak sat by Tana's head, tenderly stroking her face in the hope it might resurrect her. The compassionate gesture touched Jane and she finally shook with sobs, Tana's lifeless hand in hers.

Something warm and soft hugged her. She didn't need to open her eyes to know that Karnath had wrapped his tiny arms around her and was holding her tight.

11

News of Anil's death dropped morale further when the exhausted search party returned to Karibu Mji in the early hours of the morning. Esmée organized hot food and blankets as everybody gathered to listen to their story. The clash with Tafari's men was greeted with dark looks between the loggers. Getting any further mixed up with the insurgents was something none of them relished.

Any thoughts of heading to the town for help were quashed when Esmée told them that the jeep had stopped working. This time sabotage wasn't suspected, just the humid conditions the machinery was expected to endure. The supplies needed for the repair had all been damaged in the fire and none of the men possessed the same engineering proficiency as Robbie.

Robbie tried to press the matter of the mysterious third party holding Jane to Clark and Archie but, in their tired condition, they didn't want to speculate as to who that could be. They just hoped that Jane was alive, somewhere.

Sleep was sporadic, and Robbie kept tossing from side to side in the hammock in his tiny shack. With no air-conditioning, the room was cloyingly warm. After two hours of restless sleep, Robbie sat up and splashed bottled water over his face, but the warm water did little to refresh him. He glanced around his hut, which was empty aside from a few changes of clothes. He had no possessions, not even a photograph of his sister, as he'd never had the time or opportunity to print one and now her face was consigned only to memory; in particular the image of her lying pale and dead. Try as he might, Robbie couldn't focus on Sophie's smiling, lively face. He was left with only a nightmare for a companion.

Instead he thought of Jane. She rarely smiled, her lips usually downturned, forehead furrowed as she vented her disgust with the jungle. On the few occasions she did smile, or even more infrequently, laughed, her eyes had lit up and Robbie had seen a blonde version of his sister.

He couldn't just sit and do nothing. Running blindly into the jungle had proved to be a stupid mistake that had cost a man his life. Several times now, Archie had assured him that it wasn't his fault, but Robbie wasn't convinced by the reassurances.

Robbie gave up trying to sleep and decided to walk around the camp. It was still morning, and everybody was taking the opportunity to rest. After being in the heart of the jungle, he had grown used to the constant chitter of birds, insects, and monkeys. Here, there was nothing, not even the dull thump of the generator, which had been shut down to conserve the little fuel that hadn't been consumed by the fire.

Robbie crossed to the operations hut, a small open-sided building that looked more like a beach hut, with a counter running along one side. It was from here Clark and Archie would pay the men or assign rotations for the next few days' logging. A weather-beaten map hung on the wall, covered in black marker that highlighted their path of destruction through the rainforest.

He traced a finger from their current location, picking out Tafari's rebel base on the other side of the mountains. He frowned, wondering where their mysterious third party could be lurking. A dirt track led part of the way through a valley and from there it was a hike to the rebels' base. Multiple rivers were marked on the map, but due to the lack of detail Robbie couldn't be sure which one he had followed. He had failed to believe there could be cartographic black holes in an age of satellite mapping, but detailed maps of the region simply didn't exist.

Robbie rubbed his eyes. The area he had highlighted was vast and it was pure speculation that Jane's kidnappers were located there. He crossed over to the burnt supply hut and examined the wreckage for the first time. Three walls stood, the fourth blown outward in the same explosion that had knocked Esmée down. The roof had collapsed and it looked like the slightest breeze would topple the charred structure over. Nobody had bothered trying to salvage the contents as the remains of the crates inside were clearly burnt to a crisp.

He circled the building, looking for any clues to what had happened. The hut was at the edge of the camp; there was nothing but stumps forming a buffer zone from the jungle beyond.

Then he noticed the lantern at the foot of the supply hut. Robbie kneeled to examine it. The lanterns were powered by paraffin, which was much cheaper than batteries. They hung from poles along the periphery of the camp and gave those within some sense of the boundary; too many times had an intoxicated logger staggered into the dark fold of the jungle never to be seen again. This lantern didn't belong here, and now that Robbie was searching for it, he spotted the pole it had been removed from. It had been thrown here deliberately. Not a particularly strategic point if somebody had intended to burn the building down. Throwing it through the window would have had more immediate results. But the lantern's broken glass cover clearly indicated that it had been thrown with some force.

Mystified as to why there would be such a lackluster attack, Robbie recalled the mystery of the vanishing tree they had felled. In the confusion and drama of Jane's disappearance, he'd all but forgotten the incident.

Robbie scanned the silent trees, dead giants stripped of their foliage. He longed to go back out and search for Jane, but knew now that that was a reckless option. Robbie moved to the jeep, intending to fix it while he had nothing better to do. If he could get to the town at least he would feel as though he was doing something to save her.

As he extracted his toolbox he began to wonder if Mister David really was on to something with his talk of evil jungle spirits.

• • •

Karnath did not leave Jane's side all night. The little gorilla curled up against her in the safety of the airplane where they both slept. When she woke it was daylight again and the air had grown humid. Karnath had whined when Jane had tried to exit their shelter and she had been forced to carry him in her arms. She was surprised to discover her leg no longer hurt and she could walk freely.

The gorillas had dispersed around the lake, increasing their foraging range. Tana's body had gone, so too had Sheeta. Tarzan sat on a great root that curled around the aircraft, and jumped down when Jane waved to him.

"Hi," said Jane. She no longer felt anxious when she looked at Tarzan. He had risked his life to defend the apes, to defend her. There was no doubt in her mind that, no matter how barbaric his behavior was, Tarzan was a friend.

Tarzan didn't reply. He took Karnath, who jumped into his arms, liquid eyes looking fearfully around. Jane watched, enthralled, as Tarzan murmured gently to the ape and made a few hand gestures. She couldn't make out any words and didn't believe the gorillas could have any language skills. Nevertheless, Karnath responded with gentle grunts and a hand gesture. Jane was certain the little ape wasn't mimicking Tarzan. Not for the first time she wondered if these apes, the *Mangani* as Tarzan called them, were in fact a different, more intelligent sub-species.

"Karnath frightened," said Tarzan. "Alone."

Jane felt regret for the little ape's plight. She stroked Karnath's brow as the little ape reached for a stem of green leaves on a bush that he greedily crammed into his mouth.

"He's starving," she said with concern. "Poor little guy," she cooed as if talking to a human infant. For several minutes she fed the little ape roots and stems from the foliage around them. Jane found herself getting more concerned about his future and voiced her concerns to Tarzan.

"Karnath need new mother." For a horrible second, Jane thought he was referring to her. Then he sprang down the narrow trail, jumping from rock to tree with Karnath clinging to his chest. She could see he was heading for a knot of gorillas on the far side of the lake and hoped that one of them would look after the orphaned ape.

While Tarzan was gone, Jane thought it would be a good time to continue her search of the aircraft in a hope to find clues about Tarzan's past.

She tugged at the cargo-hold door, lending her weight to pry it open enough to allow her to slip inside.

The hold wasn't big enough to stand in and Jane was forced to crouch. She used her foot to brush aside the rusted scientific equipment that had spilt from the broken crate. She turned her attention to the two intact crates and the cloth suitcase.

The crates had previously been opened and their lids carefully replaced. Jane doubted Tarzan would have been so meticulous and wondered if D'Arnot had started to investigate his strange pupil's background. She opened one crate and discovered a stack of rusty cans. Damp had long since faded or rotted the labels, leaving their contents a mystery.

The third crate was filled with camping supplies; moldy tents, holes picked into the canvas by generations of insects, rusty poles, torn mosquito nets, and a corroded shovel.

"An expedition," Jane said to herself. "But whose?"

She examined the crates. The wood was damp and chewed in places. There were markings, but they had faded. Jane pushed the crate closer to the light, hoping to get a better look and she made out a single faint word: GREYSTOKE. The same word she'd seen in the cockpit—but what did it mean?

Maybe the suitcase would supply the answers? It was huge and Jane could just make out a faded black and gold pattern beneath the grime. The destination labels had rotted away, giving no clue to their ownership. Jane flipped the top open and immediately recoiled as dozens of black cockroaches scuttled out. She shrieked as they clambered up her arms and flooded across the floor, racing for the shadows. Jane shook them off and the insects vanished into the dark as if they had never existed.

She returned to the case and found clothes inside which were damp, musty, and chewed through; many had rotted into mulch. They looked mostly feminine, but she wasn't entirely sure. She could have sworn some of the cockroaches had burrowed deeper into the garments when she opened the case, and didn't fancy delving any further.

Then she caught a glint of silver poking out from under the sodden clothes. Taking a rusty tent pole she lifted the fabric and discovered a tarnished silver picture frame beneath. Driven by curiosity she slid a hand into the suitcase, taking hold of the frame as insects scuttled over her exposed skin.

It came loose with a soft sucking noise, black slime clinging to the bottom. Jane saw the photo of a handsome man, standing in front of a stately home. His arm was draped around a pretty young woman. Water had damaged the image, but from the hair and clothing styles Jane could tell it was taken roughly around the time she was born, maybe a few years earlier. The picture's lower half was covered with mold.

She studied the picture. As best she could tell, the man looked proud and the woman appeared content, her eyes smiling mischievously. Jane wondered if her parents had ever been so happy. As a child, she had been close to her mother—far closer than she had to Archie. When she was eleven she had taken to calling her dad "Archie" rather than "Dad" because it annoyed him and drew a smile from her mother. As Jane grew older she grew distant from Archie, but had started to notice how her mother had also become reticent toward her. Archie had later claimed that it was because her mother disliked seeing her daughter grow up, as it reminded her that she was getting old too. Jane had simply assumed her mother's erratic behavior was Archie's fault.

That was until her mother had left. Left without saying goodbye. Without warning. Without a note to explain her actions. Jane had been convinced a message would arrive and that every phone call would be her mother explaining the mystery of her disappearance. It never came. As Archie uncovered the truth, Jane increasingly refused to believe him. He'd lost count of how many times she'd called him a liar.

For weeks she had looked through the rain-soaked window of her home in Baltimore, expecting her mother's car to roll up the driveway.

That was before they lost the house. Jane had never thought that fate would lead her to the musty cargo hold of a crashed jet, stranded in the middle of the Congo jungle.

She suddenly became aware of Tarzan standing on the other side of the hold. Jane wondered how long he had been there.

"Come," said Tarzan in his usual conversational manner.

Jane debated showing him the picture, but doubted it would mean anything to him. She dropped it back in the case and followed Tarzan outside.

Squinting her eyes against the sun, she asked, "Where's Karnath?"

Tarzan led her along the wingtip that extended from the cliff, over the lake below. He pointed to the foot of the waterfall, across the caldera. Jane could see the tiny gorilla was playing with other youngsters under the watchful supervision of Kerchak.

"Now we find food," said Tarzan. His tongue was still thick around the syllables when he spoke, but Jane could detect an improvement in his speech.

"Where are we going?" she asked. She no longer felt in such a rush to return to Karibu Mji. The photograph had stirred nostalgic memories of happier times back home. Times that were now lost forever.

As she watched Karnath play with the other young apes she began to feel a connection to the jungle. Standing on the wing overlooking the Eden-like valley, she felt her previous hostility toward the jungle had vanished. It was as harsh and cruel as the civilized world, but it could also be simple and beautiful. The air was clear, the soft thrum of the waterfall was soothing, the colors were more vibrant than anything she could remember, and her companion was not the bloodthirsty cannibal she had initially assumed.

There was no complicated relationship with Archie to stress her out nor was Tarzan trying to turn the jungle into a barren wilderness.

"Swim," said Tarzan with a mischievous grin.

Jane frowned, then she followed his gaze down. She was standing *over* the lake, the blue-green water sparkling in the sunlight below—130 feet below. She instinctively stepped back, but felt Tarzan's vice-like grip on her arm. He was still smiling.

"I—I can't jump," stammered Jane who had feared diving boards since her swimming lessons in school. The height of this dwarfed those memories. "I don't like—"

Tarzan clearly didn't want to know. Jane felt a sharp tug on her arm and experienced a sense of being thrust forward. Her legs turned to jelly, but she no longer needed them—Tarzan had pushed her off the edge.

Jane plummeted feet first. She had no time to scream. Tarzan soared alongside, falling headfirst, arms extended to break the water as the roar of wind filled her senses. She wanted to close her eyes but they were fixed on the lake rushing toward them.

Tarzan hit the water first—barely making a ripple. Jane hit it with a terrific splash. She felt the shock of cold water as she plunged beneath the surface. Her legs kicked out, but didn't stop her descent. Her ears hurt with the pressure and the world was filled with bubbles and whitewater and she lost sense of what direction she was facing. She was convinced her legs would shatter against the rocky lakebed.

Instead, she suddenly found herself swiftly rising back up as her natural buoyancy took over. Instinct powered her legs and arms, and she broke the surface gulping deep breaths of air.

Tarzan treaded the water next to her, a smug look on his face.

"You total idiot! You pushed me! How . . . How could you . . .? You . . . you didn't even know if I could swim! I could have drowned . . ." she trailed off. Tarzan was laughing, his face scrunched up as if she had told him the funniest joke he'd ever heard. The sound of Tarzan's laughter reverberated off the cliff wall and with it Jane's temper melted away. What was the point in getting angry? Tarzan had pushed her off the cliff, over a drop she would never have dared contemplate before. But she had survived.

Now she felt more alive than ever before. Tarzan's infectious guffaws got to her and she began howling with laughter. Tensions melted away, replaced by an urge to make the leap again. From the violence of the previous night to the exhilaration of the morning, being alive had never felt so good and she had never felt so free.

Tarzan and Jane swam from the lake and followed the river downstream. She couldn't keep up with his powerful strokes, but he patiently waited for her and never complained. When she felt tired, Jane would roll on to her back and drift with the current. With Tarzan close by, she wasn't worried about any predators lurking to take a bite out of her.

Jane didn't know how long they spent drifting down the river watching the green landscape as they passed by. On several occasions the current picked up and the water turned white as they were swept between boulders. Rather than swim for the bank, Tarzan crossed his arms over his chest and shot through the chasm feet first. Jane apprehensively followed his lead and they raced through whitewater sections of the river like torpedoes, never once careening into the giant boulders on either side.

Despite these occasional rapids it was a pleasant, relaxing experience. The river became wider and Tarzan drifted for the shore. Jane followed, worried he had spotted some danger ahead. Tarzan was crouched on the bank, half in the water, poised like an Olympic sprinter. He stared hard into the bamboo towering over them. The forest floor was lost in a mass of thick vegetation. She couldn't see anything to be alarmed about.

"What is it?" she whispered.

"Food," Tarzan answered in a low voice. On cue, Jane's stomach rumbled, reminding her that she hadn't eaten since the previous day. Tarzan gave her a reproachful look—then suddenly bolted into the thicket.

Jane saw the vegetation violently move as Tarzan's quarry fled. Tarzan moved with great speed and utter surefootedness. He gracefully leapt against the thick bamboo—bouncing from one to another to propel himself upward, over the bushes. Jane had only seen such acrobatics in martial-arts movies and had been convinced the actors were suspended on wires.

Tarzan utilized his momentum to perform the stunning feat without a moment's thought. He disappeared into the jungle, then suddenly emerged chasing an antelope that was only a few feet ahead of him. Jane suddenly realized that he was working his prey toward the river.

An antelope sped from the bushes straight for Jane. The animal saw her and panicked. It tried to turn—and that was the moment that Tarzan leapt, grappling its hind legs and bringing the creature splashing down into the shallows of the river. It thrashed around, but Tarzan kept a tight hold, avoiding the long horns as the animal shook its head.

"What are you doing?" screamed Jane as Tarzan drew his dagger. She looked away too late and saw the blade slit the bushbuck's throat. Tarzan he wore a steely grin of triumph.

Jane refused to cry—she was too tough for that—but she tried not to look at the bloody carcass as Tarzan carried it over and dropped it in front of her.

"Food!" he said with a smile.

"You are disgusting!" she spat with contempt. "How could you kill an innocent . . ." her words trailed away as Tarzan slit the animal's stomach open with the knife. Jane could feel the bile rising in her throat, her appetite vanquished. Tarzan leaned down and tore a strip of raw flesh from the antelope. He chewed on it happily, offering a chunk to Jane, who recoiled. "How could you do that?"

"Tarzan hungry," he said and ripped another piece of flesh from the animal.

"It's barbaric!"

"Jane not eat meat?"

"Jane *do* eat meat. Cooked meat that comes from a packet!"

Tarzan nodded thoughtfully. "What animal is packet?"

"It's not an animal, it's what the meat comes in. The meat comes from . . ." she trailed off. Back in Baltimore, her best friend, Hazel Strong, had once denounced meat and tried to persuade Jane to become a vegetarian. Hazel had described, in grotesque detail, how the animals were killed. Jane had tried it for a whole two days before succumbing to a burger. From what Hazel had told her, Tarzan's method of killing was much more humane.

"Eat," insisted Tarzan.

Jane stared at the warm flesh. There was no way she could bring herself to do it. The smell alone was revolting.

"I'll find some fruit," she said, trying to hide her revulsion. She glanced up and saw a pair of vultures circling. Their arrival had been almost instantaneous.

Tarzan sat back contentedly after he had eaten, allowing the vultures to move in, noisily quarrelling over the carcass. A short while later, Tarzan indicated they should leave. They walked down the bank and Jane glanced back at the dead bushbuck.

"Shouldn't we bury it?"

"The dead keep the land alive," he replied pointing to the vultures.

The riverbank became impassable so they returned to the water to swim onward. As they drifted down the bank she wondered what had made him endure this life? Why hadn't he tried to find civilization? His loathing for mankind's desire to kill itself was evident. Had Tarzan really found solace out here?

The current became swift again and they shot through the occasional narrow stretch of whitewater. Jane whooped with delight as they sped through, once again reminded how wonderful it felt to be alive.

The last stretch of rapids sent them over the edge of a moderate-sized waterfall. Jane somersaulted through the air before vanishing into the curtain of mist at the foot of the fall's plunge pool. She was disorientated, but this time she relaxed and allowed her body to rise naturally to the surface. She surfaced and saw that Tarzan was already ashore and plucking fruits from a tree that bent low over the water.

A small group of dark brown L'Hoest's monkeys, sporting fluffy white beards and long slender tails, sat on the bank paying attention to Tarzan. The monkeys ate fruit from the ground, a few of them running to catch plum specimens Tarzan plucked and tossed to them.

Jane noisily waded to the shore and the monkeys panicked—howling and running for the safety of the large boulders. Jane wrung out her shirt and hair, watching the monkeys as they bared their teeth.

"What's their problem?"

"You." Tarzan handed her a large green fruit. "Jane make noise like Tantor!"

Jane bit into the fruit. It tasted vaguely of avocado and suddenly reminded her how hungry she was. Between bites she asked, "What's Tantor?"

Tarzan looked puzzled. He tried to think of another way to say it, but instead shrugged. "Tantor is Tantor."

"That helps a lot," quipped Jane sarcastically and picked a fruit off the floor, fussily wiping the dirt onto her shirt. That seemed to amuse Tarzan, who took one and bit into it, dirt and all.

"Jane always angry, never see. Never listen."

Jane rolled her eyes. He was beginning to sound like her father. "What's there to see? A few monkeys and a bunch of trees."

Tarzan grunted, a cross between a human scoff and a gorilla grunt of annoyance. "Look! Listen!"

She sighed. "OK, whatever. What am I listening f—"

Tarzan clamped a hand over her mouth, then cocked his head to the trees around them. Jane decided to play along and listened. The waterfall thundered close by, almost drowning out the birds twittering in the canopy above them. The monkeys made small grunts as they foraged for berries, keeping their distance from Jane. She tried to speak but Tarzan kept his hand in place. She continued listening. Focusing. After a while she discovered she could peel back the layers of sounds and tune them out. She closed her eyes and Tarzan removed his hand. She now heard the monkeys all the more vividly. Then she became aware of her own breathing. She had never realized just how noisy she was. She strained to listen for Tarzan but could hear nothing.

She was concentrating so hard that she almost gasped when the monkeys' intonations changed from contentment to terse, wary coughs. She tilted her head and picked out another noise: the faintest crunch of leaves. She pinpointed the direction the noise was coming from and opened her eyes. Tarzan was already looking the same way, as were the L'Hoest's monkeys.

Farther down the bank the foliage gently parted and a brown giraffe-like head poked out, scanning the area for danger. Jane remained perfectly still as the animal stepped out and bent to drink from the river. It was the size of a horse, with a white head that abruptly turned into a brown coat. Jane thought she was in a dream when she noticed the front and rear legs were stripped like a zebra. Jane remembered a story Esmée was fond of telling her about her great-great-grandfather, who had had a pet okapi in his youth, long before science "discovered" it in 1901. Jane was looking at a very rare animal.

The okapi glanced in their direction, twitched its large ears, and then continued drinking. Tarzan watched the animal with respect and Jane found it difficult to equate his obvious love of the jungle with the feral hunter inside him.

She wondered how Tarzan would cope back in the real world.

12

Tafari was angry. Bapoto flinched when the guerrilla leader kicked a folding metal table off the porch and it clanged against the side of a jeep.

"You let those peasants take everything!" Tafari snarled, stabbing his cigar in their direction. "Your weapons, your honor . . . you're not men of the FDLR, you are animals!"

Bapoto sensibly avoided making eye contact. Tafari had been known to execute his men if the news they brought was not to his liking.

"There were dozens of them," Bapoto lied. He glanced at his men who all stood to attention, staring at a spot over Tafari's head. They had agreed to conceal the truth during the long hike back. "They took us by surprise."

"But they did not kill you," barked Tafari. That was a cardinal sin in his book. His band of rebels only had one future, to die in combat. Of course, Tafari didn't include himself in that. He had been fighting for Hutu Power all his life. It was a caste war that had led to genocide in Rwanda. Tafari had commanded many murderous bands responsible for countless vile atrocities and he had enjoyed every one of them. His was one of several militia groups that could no longer stay in Rwanda when peace had settled and was the first to run into battle during the Second Congo War.

Now wanted for genocide, Tafari had nowhere to go, and no wars left to fight. He had only his survival and so had fled with his men into the jungle. He now led his men with one goal—to accumulate wealth. Tafari reasoned that, if he could gather enough money, he could assume a new identity and leave the oppressive jungle behind. Running protection rackets for the various illegal activities around his patch of jungle was lucrative. He had no idea why the American loggers chose to provoke him, but when the two heads of the operation came barging into his camp days earlier, he knew they were looking for trouble.

Tafari was good at trouble. He was also paranoid and was beginning to suspect the loggers were not who they appeared to be.

Tafari folded his arms behind his back and paced across the porch, looking every bit the dictator general he was. Thick cigar smoke coiled around his head. "We need to teach them a lesson they will not forget!"

"Yes, sir," responded Bapoto dutifully. "We will burn their camp to the ground!"

Tafari thought about that. It would be a shame because the loggers were providing a good income for him. Killing them would be a powerful warning to others, yet . . . he was certain he could find a better use for them. Perhaps the Americans had personal fortunes he could plunder? But first, he wanted to get to the root of why they provoked him.

It had been a long time since he had organized a large raiding party. He was getting excited about the prospect of the bloodshed ahead.

• • •

The atmosphere at Karibu Mji was still somber and Archie felt as though they were facing a revolt. He stood on the bonnet of the jeep, which Robbie had almost got working again with many improvised parts. Clark sat in the driver's seat, chin propped on the wheel. The fourteen remaining loggers stood around them, led by Mister David.

"They want to get back to work," said Mister David reasonably.

The crowd murmured their agreement.

"Right now my daughter is the priority!"

"She is lost!" shouted Serge. Archie felt his blood boil. "We looked and found no trace!"

Mister David caught the expression on his boss's face. "Mr. Porter, we stand with you. We like Jane. We looked for Jane. But we found only death. You cannot expect us to look in every tree in the Congo to find her."

"If that's what it takes," Archie snapped back.

An angry clamor arose from the men. Hands were flicked in gestures for him to shut up.

Clark stood on the seat. "Listen, all of ya. You're here to be paid. That's what you want, that's what we want. There ain't no argument. All we ask is that *when* we know where Jane is, we can turn to you for help."

The tone of the crowd changed. Clark was satisfied with the nodding of heads. He saw Robbie and Esmée watching from the open classroom.

"What the hell are you doing?" hissed Archie, turning to Clark so nobody could overhear.

"Stoppin' our workforce from walkin' out," replied Clark calmly. "We can't afford to keep payin' them to sit around."

"What about Jane? I'm not giving up!" Archie growled.

"Nor am I, mate. I'm just stoppin' us having a full-on rebellion here."

Archie wanted to argue but Mister David spoke up, loud enough to make the crowd lapse into silence.

"That sounds good enough." He turned to the workers. "Come with me for your work assignments."

Mister David led the crowd to the office, and began issuing orders, pointing out the valuable areas they should concentrate on.

Archie was incredulous. He jumped from the bonnet intending to plead with them to help search for his daughter, but he knew Clark was right. No matter how much it hurt.

Clark climbed from the vehicle. "Listen, mate. We got one man dead 'cause of this. If that lot walk away we lose everythin.'"

"I can't just sit here and do nothing." Archie had intended the comment to sound angry, but it came out in a deflated wheeze. Jane was all he had left in the world and it was a monumental struggle not to break down in tears. Several times he had resolved to march back out into the wilderness and not return until he found her. Each time he had talked himself out of the suicidal venture as he imagined Jane returning home, and the look on her face knowing her father had sacrificed himself for her. It was an emotional conundrum that Archie didn't have the strength to untangle.

Clark broke his cyclical thoughts. "We won't. Robbie's almost got the jeep workin'. He'll go to town and raise the alarm and get help from the rangers."

"What kind of help?" Archie knew their chances of finding Jane were slipping away by the hour.

"He'll do what he can," said Clark. It was the only answer he could supply without giving false hope to his friend. "Who knows, maybe Jane's found her way there already? She's a smart girl."

Archie nodded, unable to look him in the eye. He walked back to his shack, preferring to be alone with his own accusing conscience.

• • •

Robbie felt angry when he saw Archie retreat to his cabin and Clark join the workers as they hauled tools and headed for the trees.

"They've given up," he said darkly.

Esmée nodded sadly, then turned her attention back to the map they had laid across two desks. It was the same as the one hanging in the office, but this was covered in pencil markings Esmée had made.

"Tafari controls this area here." She circled a portion of the map that included Karibu Mji. "There's a coltan mine 'bout here. They diggin' that stuff for your mobile phones and don't care 'bout the mess they leave behind." She marked off a small area at the base of the mountains that stood between Tafari's camp and Karibu Mji. It was within the area Robbie had highlighted down on the map.

"Would miners have taken her?"

"You know Archie and Clark went through this already? They don't think so."

"They may have missed something," said Robbie keeping his eyes on the map.

Esmée looked at him with pity. "You know they now think she gone 'n' got lost? Nobody believes she was taken."

"I do," said Robbie firmly.

Esmée sighed. "Miners keep quiet. Out of Tafari's hair best they can. But things change like. Used to all be 'bout power. Now it's 'bout greed."

"What about poachers?"

Esmée laughed humorlessly. "They get everywhere." She gestured to the map. "My boys found snares when they been lookin' to fill our cookin' pots. They generally cowards."

Robbie remembered one man had suffered a nasty injury when he went on a hunting expedition with Mister David. He had blindly stumbled into a trap intended to catch bushmeat.

Robbie was running out of options. Maybe Archie's grim theory was correct? He looked at Esmée and slouched, defeated.

"You don't believe I'm right, do you?"

"I don't think it's no poachers took her," said Esmée shaking her head.

Robbie detected the unusual way she'd said that. "Who did then?"

Esmée smiled. She was an educated woman and knew Robbie would instantly scoff at any suggestion of the supernatural. However, Esmée was wise enough never to discount anything at face value. She believed there were many creatures out there still waiting to be discovered. Over the years she had witnessed many a scientific party find new plants, insects, fish, birds, lizards, and even mammals.

"Who did?" repeated Robbie impatiently.

Esmée sighed. "You gotta broaden your mind, Mister Canler. Open it to unusual possibilities."

Robbie harrumphed and rubbed his eyes. He was still fatigued and in no mood to listen to superstitious theories. "Please, Esmée. You of all people? The ghost?"

Esmée's dark eyes studied him. "The White Ape. I seen it. Afore I come here. Saw it in the trees, watchin'. . ." There was a faraway look in her eyes as she recalled. "Didn't think it meant no harm." She looked directly at Robbie and smiled. "I believe Jane is safe."

Robbie quickly folded the map up and slipped it into his back pocket. He gave Esmée a disapproving look. "Well, I don't and I'm not going to stop looking for her." He stomped toward the jeep, intent on fixing it before nightfall. He didn't know what he could do, but he was determined not to stop searching for Jane.

• • •

As the sun climbed in the sky, Tarzan had had enough of the river and beckoned for Jane to follow him into the canopy. He easily caromed between a pair of trunks and shot up the tree. Jane tried to replicate his actions but ended up flat on her back, laughing hard.

She clambered up the tree, grasping at every handhold. It was slow going and Tarzan watched with an unimpressed yawn. After several minutes of scrambling, Tarzan grew bored and hoisted her up the branches with a single arm. On the relative safety of a wide branch he demonstrated leaping from slender limb to crooked branch. He made it look easy with his perfect sense of balance.

Jane silently girded herself, then skipped to a nearby branch as he had done. It was less than two feet away but she landed with flailing arms and felt herself toppling forward. Tarzan's reassuring hand grabbed her by the scruff of her shirt and set her upright.

"You think too much," he said, tapping his head. Jane laughed, not quite following his meaning. "Trust movements. Be strong."

He jumped to another branch without any effort and beckoned her to follow. Jane watched fearfully—it was a longer jump than last time. The ground was only twelve feet away, but it was enough to break a limb or kill her if she landed on her head. She licked her lips and tried to put the negative thoughts out of her mind. She focused on the jump, visualizing exactly where she would land. Then she ran for it.

Jane sprang over the gap and landed perfectly. The branch swayed violently from the impact. She crouched, gripping the wood tightly and the bucking limb came to a gentle stop. She slowly stood, arms stretched out like a tightrope walker, relieved that she'd actually done it.

Tarzan was keen to continue the lesson and for Jane it felt as if they were in the trees for hours, jumping from one trunk to another. Every time she lost her balance, Tarzan was there to help her. Little by little she was improving, as a confidence that she'd never known she possessed took control. Compared to Tarzan she was a lumbering infant, but her fear of falling was soon replaced by adrenalin as they climbed higher in the canopy.

She followed Tarzan to a branch that curled sharply up like a "U" and provided a secure place to sit, her bare feet dangling sixty feet above the ground. She prodded her soles. They were becoming calloused and hard as they adapted to the rigors of the jungle.

Tarzan peered from the tree, his brow furrowed against the sun. He didn't move, apart from his nostrils, which flared as he sniffed the air. Jane was thoughtful as she watched him.

"Does the name 'Greystoke' mean anything to you?" Tarzan didn't respond. She wondered if it was a person, place, or a company. "What do you remember about coming to the jungle?"

Tarzan broke his gaze and looked at her for a long moment. "There was nothing before. Tarzan always here. Come."

He started to move, then doubled back for Jane. He placed her arms around his neck and mimed she should hold tight.

"Where are we going?"

"Down."

Jane couldn't get her next question out before Tarzan jumped from the tree. She screamed. It felt like freefall as branches furiously whipped past them. Tarzan clutched at them for a second before they were torn from his hand, slowing them down until he could grip a sturdy bough. They swung around it in a complete circle before Tarzan let go and landed like a cat, using both arms and legs to cushion the fall. Jane ungraciously slipped from his back and splashed into soft mud.

"OW! What were you thinking?" she said, spitting mud from her mouth. She stood up and waggled a finger at Tarzan. "What was so urgent that you . . ." Her voice trailed off as she followed his gaze.

They stood on the banks of a river. She couldn't claim it was familiar because they all looked the same to her. The mound of earth Tarzan was looking at was obviously man-made. A bamboo cross lay flat on the ground. It had fallen when some animal had started digging the dirt away to get to the flesh beneath.

Tarzan approached without any signs of fear and Jane reluctantly followed. She caught a glimpse of the corpse and quickly looked away. But that glimpse had been enough to burn into her memory. The corpse's head and upper torso had been uncovered and half chewed by a jungle scavenger. Insects crawled over the body and Jane now fully understood Tarzan's ambiguous statement about the dead helping the living. She was also certain she recognized the semi-devoured face as one of the loggers.

An overwhelming sense of guilt struck her. She had been lost in a world of natural wonder, so driven to try to understand who Tarzan was and how he had ended up here that she'd lost sight of the fact that her father must be worried to death. People were searching for her and the dead man indicated some had even died because of it.

"You've got to take me back," she suddenly said.

Tarzan made no effort to cover the dead man with dirt. A day ago, Jane would have thought that was because he possessed no human emotions. Now she understood it was because that's the way things were in the jungle—another forager would simply uncover the body again.

"Home?" said Tarzan.

Jane hesitated. From his tone, she understood he meant with his band of apes. While she no longer feared him, Jane was still unsure if he would allow her to leave.

"*My* home. The camp where I lived with my father."

Tarzan snarled. "Murderers!"

"No!"

"Kill trees, kill jungle. Tarzan's jungle," growled Tarzan with a wild look in his eyes.

Jane took a step toward him, determined not to show fear. Strength was a quality Tarzan respected and understood so she laid a firm hand on his arm.

"They don't mean to do that. They just don't understand. I can talk to them, I promise. My father's a good man. He doesn't mean you any harm."

Tarzan looked at Jane for a long moment. He nodded and his exasperation was replaced by sadness.

"Jane leave. Jane not come back."

"Of course I'll come back!" She would have said anything to see her father again, but as she spoke the words she was surprised to realize she meant them. In the space of two nights Jane's opinion of the jungle had changed. It was hostile, unforgiving, but it was also beautiful and amazing. She couldn't find the words to describe her mixed feelings.

"D'Arnot left. Not come back."

"I'll come back to see you. I'm not going to die!" She regretted the clumsy comment the moment she said it, but Tarzan didn't react. "I need to know if my father's OK. He'll be missing me."

Tarzan nodded in understanding and for a fleeting moment, Jane saw a vulnerable, handsome young man beneath his impossibly muscular body. He had endured hardships she couldn't imagine and now she was about to abandon him. Once again, Jane's feelings were in turmoil. She couldn't bear to see the sadness on Tarzan's face so she forced a smile and squeezed his arm. It was like clutching concrete.

"Tarzan . . . you've saved me a dozen times already. You're my friend."

Tarzan smiled, gripping her shoulder hard enough to bruise. Jane bore the pain with a smile.

"You Tarzan's friend."

"So you'll take me back?" asked Jane rubbing her shoulder.

Tarzan nodded then cupped his hands around his mouth and bellowed a long-drawn-out bass. The birds and monkeys ceased their chatter and the forest fell deathly silent. Tarzan cocked his head this way and that in search of a response. Then he roared again.

A deeper call reply echoed through the trees. Tarzan smiled and called again. He was answered almost immediately. Now Jane could hear the snapping of branches as something approached. Something big.

Tarzan looked at the trees expectantly and Jane hated herself for cowering slightly behind him.

"What is it?" she whispered.

Louder cracks as wood was torn underfoot. Jane watched with wide eyes as the trees shook, leaves cascading from their boughs. The ground trembled and Tarzan grinned.

"Tantor!"

A huge elephant trotted from the jungle, trees parting around it.

On seeing Tarzan it let out a huge trumpet and reared on to its hind legs before splashing down in the shallow waters of the river's edge. Tarzan ran to Tantor and stroked its trunk as the animal thrust it into the water to drink.

Jane could hear Tarzan making soothing sounds as he scratched the mighty forest elephant's rounded ear. The elephant's jaw was long and narrow, with a pair of short tusks pointing down. Tantor didn't seem worried when Jane approached and ran a hand over his flank. It felt like tough leather with fine hairs dispersed across it.

"Hello Tantor," she said. The elephant was huge, much larger than forest elephants usually grew. Now she understood how Tarzan had managed to steal a freshly hewn tree in the dead of night.

"Tantor will take you home," said Tarzan patting the beast's flank. He barked a guttural command and the elephant crooked his knee. Tarzan used that to hoist Jane onto Tantor's back, then jumped up and sat behind her. He belched another nonsensical command, and the great pachyderm began marching along the riverbank.

Once Jane had got used to the unusual swaying sensation, she started to enjoy the ride. There was no need for Tarzan to guide the animal, as he was familiar with every path through the jungle. Tantor left the riverbank and pushed along trails in the undergrowth that Jane would have thought were too narrow for such bulk, but Tantor took each step with care. Many times Tarzan and Jane were forced to duck as they passed under low-hanging branches.

The sun cruised across the sky and Tantor often stopped to pick some delicacy from the forest floor or trees as they passed, using his prehensile trunk to pluck the morsels. During those times, Tarzan would reach out and pull fruits from the trees. Jane began to wonder just how long her stomach could stand a fruit diet.

After a while she felt her eyes begin to close as Tantor's gentle motion lulled her to sleep. A few times she woke to find she was leaning against Tarzan, but she felt secure enough to doze almost instantly as fatigue gripped her.

Jane had no idea how long had passed when she was awoken as Tantor splashed across the river. The water came to the bottom of Jane's feet, but they were soon across.

They continued on as the sun sank below the horizon and cast its last golden hue over the land. She turned to speak to Tarzan but was surprised to discover he wasn't there. She looked around in confusion. Had he fallen? Tantor didn't seem to have noticed as he plowed through the undergrowth and emerged in a wide clearing. Dozens of people stared at her in disbelief as the elephant came to a stop. It was now too dark to make out any faces.

"Jane?"

Jane recognized Robbie's voice as he pushed through the awed loggers. His face was lit with a broad smile.

"JANE'S BACK!" he yelled.

Archie bolted from his shack and stared at his daughter astride the elephant with momentary shock before he raced forward.

Tantor raised his knee, allowing Jane to step down and she ran into the crushing embrace of her father. He didn't say a word, instead he cried with relief.

Robbie ruffled her hair and treated her to a sheepish grin. "We missed ya."

Clark squeezed her arm. "Welcome back, kiddo."

Jane was overwhelmed with emotions from the reunion and welcomed her father's embrace for several long minutes.

Robbie looked her up and down. "Are you OK? What happened?"

Jane playfully punched his arm. "Of course I'm all right. Thanks. You won't believe where I've been!"

She turned to introduce Tantor—but the elephant had silently vanished back into the jungle. Jane turned to follow, hoping to see Tarzan standing at the tree line, but now the jungle once again looked dark and foreboding.

Her gaze swept the trees as arms wrapped around her and she was guided to the bar, numerous voices asking questions.

She couldn't spot Tarzan and wondered if that was the last she would see of her mysterious savior.

13

Two days had passed since Jane's return and the camp had settled back to normality. Jane's story about being saved by the strange man who lived with gorillas was greeted with polite nods and smiles. She couldn't help but notice the skeptical looks that passed between her listeners. It didn't take long for her to realize she wasn't being taken seriously.

Mister David told her that it was not unknown for pygmy tribes in the jungle to look after strangers. He thought it likely the Mbuti people had cared for her while she was injured and spoke with confidence that, in a feverish state, their unusual appearance would have confused Jane. When she showed the wound on her leg, stitched with ant heads, it only served to prove Mister David's point. He seemed desperate not to believe his *Negoogunogumbar* could be a man.

It rapidly became apparent to Jane that everybody was willing to believe natives had cared for her rather than stories of a wild man who lived with the apes. After all, she must have been through a lot of stress. As long as she was safe, the truth didn't seem to matter. Even her own father shushed her when she tried to speak of her adventure, and advised her to rest. Robbie asked her a few questions but she could see the disbelief in his eyes and at one point he scoffed at the idea of a man living with a band of gorillas. She later saw him talking quietly to Mister David, casting concerned glances in her direction. She caught the words *trauma* and *delusional* and resolved to stop speaking about her experience.

She found life at Karibu Mji to be more of a bore than she remembered. In fact, she found it an appalling place to be. The dead wood and gasoline fumes were at complete odds with the vibrant jungle she had experienced.

Before meeting Tarzan she had no idea what wonders the jungle held, but now she was back to being a part of their destruction.

The only welcome additions were hot water, clean clothes, and the hot meals Esmée prepared, although Jane did prod the meat in the stew thoughtfully as she wondered what animal it had come from.

She had been impressed by how much she had remembered from her lessons about life in the jungle and had pressed Esmée to reveal everything she knew about the jungle's mysteries. Her teacher gently assured her that lessons would be suspended until she was feeling better.

Robbie had tried to get her interested in helping him fix the jeep, which was proving to be a tough problem without the correct spare parts. Jane sat with him for a few hours, but watching Robbie repair the engine and getting covered in oil held no appeal.

Archie kept a close eye on her and soon Jane was beginning to feel uncomfortable with the omnipresent surveillance. Robbie had returned her iPhone, which was now working, despite the numerous dunks it had taken. The screen was damaged but she thought she could still type her thoughts in another email to Hazel, knowing full well it would never be sent.

Sitting on a stump at the edge of the encampment she stared at the blank email, but inspiration to chronicle her time in the jungle refused to come. She no longer felt the desire to complain about her life. Something had changed inside her, but she wasn't sure exactly what. She put the phone away and stared at the dead trees that formed a barrier between their little town and the beguiling jungle beyond. She peered curiously into the darkness beyond. A quick glance behind revealed

Robbie had stopped tinkering with the engine and was watching her. She turned back to the trees and spoke in a low voice.

"Tarzan? Are you there?"

There was no reply. She scanned the trees for any signs of life, half hoping Tantor would come blustering out of the bush. But there was nothing.

• • •

Robbie watched Jane as she stared at the trees. He felt sorry for her—she must be feeing terribly confused to have spouted the nonsensical stories she had.

As the second day wore on, Robbie could see Jane was becoming reserved and listless. He was worried she might be suffering from an infection, but there was nothing they could do for her in the camp. They had to get Jane to the nearest town.

Robbie focused his attention on the jeep's engine. He had used a small pocketknife to whittle some improvised parts in place and finally reassembled it. He slipped the knife into his pocket and turned the ignition. After a few spluttering starts the vehicle rumbled to life. Satisfied with his handiwork, he finally confided in Archie.

"I think she needs to see a doctor," he said, then quickly corrected himself, remembering Archie's past. "One with antibiotics."

He sat with Archie and Esmée in the empty bar. Clark was out wrangling the men and Jane now never came inside if she could help it. Archie drummed his fingers on the wooden bar.

"Sleeping sickness, maybe," said Esmée, who had also noticed Jane's change in behavior.

"*Trypanosomiasis*," said Archie, recalling his medical training. "It could be weeks or months for any symptoms to show. But she says she has no infected bites. I'm more worried about her leg. That's a nasty scar and whatever the natives gave her, I'd feel better if we can get her some antibiotics. Amoxicillin will do. I also think she's still in shock. Last night she even asked me to stop logging. Asked—not shouted."

Esmée didn't respond. She could see the damage the logging was causing, but she needed the job.

Robbie frowned. "And then what would we do?" He felt protective of the expedition. He still needed a lot more money to start the new life he dreamed of and had several years of toil ahead of him.

"That's exactly what I said to her. She just got upset and stormed out."

"The girl needs time away from 'ere," said Esmée. "It's 'nough to drive anybody crazy." Archie looked offended. "Well, it is! Ain't no place for her. I'm not talkin' 'bout a holiday. Just a day to the town maybe. Do her good."

Robbie nodded enthusiastically. Now Jane was back safe and sound, his concern had turned to his own problems. The last thing he wanted was Jane spreading ideas about closing down the logging operation. He half believed Archie would do it if it meant keeping his daughter safe.

"Now I've got the jeep running I can go for supplies. She can come with me."

Archie wasn't sure. The idea of sending two Americans to the town wasn't very appealing. He was trying to make sure they kept a low profile.

"Mister David usually does the run."

"But you need him here since we're so far behind our quota. And I'd have to go because if the jeep breaks down again, I'm the only one who can fix it." Robbie tried not to sound desperate but this was a chance to break away from Clark's shadow and prove his value to the camp.

Archie rubbed his chin stubble; he liked Robbie's determination. It reminded him of how he'd behaved when he was younger.

Robbie dropped in his trump card. "They have a charity outpost there with a doctor. I can make sure they look at her."

Archie squinted at Robbie, weighing him up. He eventually smiled and nodded his consent.

• • •

Since commanding Tantor to deliver Jane to her home, Tarzan had taken to the trees and kept vigil. He didn't trust the band of loggers and could not understand Jane's insistence on returning to them. There were many encampments hidden under the vast, verdant canopy and almost every one had offended Tarzan by despoiling the land, slashing and burning the forest, and butchering animals—not for food but as trophies. He had traveled far and wide, and had encountered urban towns and war zones, but the smells and activity had warned him away. Occasionally he came across small groups of travelers who only seemed to want to observe nature. These he let pass, although he kept a wary eye on them.

He had watched as Jane's tribe protectively gathered around her and she appeared happy to be amongst her own people. In the following days, Tarzan prowled around the logging operation. During daylight hours he kept to the safety of the trees, but at night he would sneak across the camp's lantern boundary to investigate further. An armed sentinel patrolled the base, a shotgun lazily cradled in his arm. Tarzan knew about these inhumane weapons and had considered attacking the guard, but refrained because he was a member of Jane's tribe. Instead, he set about mischievous tasks. He would use sticks to wedge doors closed, trapping their occupants inside. Ribbons, used by the loggers to mark trails, would vanish or be set up to form a circular path. Tarzan would take great delight in watching the loggers' faces as they realized they'd walked back into the camp they'd just left. He also enjoyed their expressions of fear as they glanced at the trees.

He watched Jane, and was disappointed that she made no effort to enter the jungle. Her friend was always at her side; he had caught the name Robbie several times. Even though Robbie smelled of oil and steel, odors that Tarzan found offensive, he knew she was safe and he began to realize his first thought had been correct: She wasn't going to return. He felt this with a deep sadness, the same disconsolation he had felt when D'Arnot had left him to head back to civilization. Even then, Tarzan had known that he was being abandoned and would never see his friend again. He was proved right when he discovered D'Arnot's body weeks later. What had happened to the Frenchman in the interim remained a mystery to Tarzan.

Even with Jane amongst them, he couldn't ignore the fact the tribe was destroying his kingdom. Many times he could barely control his rage as they felled the ancient trees. By the second day, his anger was escalating and he knew he must leave before he drew blood. But he still felt the urge to pay the loggers one last visit. It wasn't difficult to follow their trail of destruction—a channel of trees had been cut down, the undergrowth beneath burnt clear so the loggers could drag the timber to the river.

From his vantage point, Tarzan was outraged at the new swathe of deforestation. His nostrils detected burnt flesh, and he found the coiled body of an armored giant pangolin, a funny creature that ate ants and did little else but amuse Tarzan. The poor creature must have been sleeping when it was burnt alive. Even for this unintended death, Tarzan was outraged and saw red—and his anger goaded him into taking risks. Despite the loyalty he felt toward Jane he could not let the loggers go unpunished.

In broad daylight he had stalked the loggers as they rolled a log into the river, made all the more difficult since Tarzan had sabotaged their large yellow machine. The river was now choked with floating trunks that needed to be shepherded downstream. Tarzan picked out the team leader, the sunburnt one they called Archie. He would kill him first.

Tarzan was outnumbered, but doubted the weaker men could defeat him. A chainsaw lay behind one logger. Tarzan had seen the noisy blades chew effortlessly through wood and wondered what effect they would have on flesh. This machine was silent, but Tarzan would make it roar.

He took the chainsaw... then hesitated. By the time a logger turned to retrieve the saw, Tarzan was back under cover with the weapon. He had not forgotten Jane's words that this tribe was not evil, but he still didn't fully understand. However, her words had had some effect. Would killing these people really stop the destruction? More would come to replace them.

Tarzan examined the chainsaw but couldn't see how to bring it to life so he threw it into the river. This time killing was not the answer. He hoped Jane would stay true to her promise and persuade them to leave peacefully.

• • •

At first, Jane had refused the offer to travel to the village with Robbie. He was surprised, as she'd previously have jumped at the chance to leave the camp. He didn't want to mention his ulterior motive of getting her to the doctor, so instead he cajoled her by reminding her that there was an Internet connection. As he'd thought she would, Jane changed her mind and agreed to accompany him.

The drive along the red jungle track was arduous. Even with the jeep's modified suspension the vehicle jolted from side to side, tossing them into the doors, which kept threatening to open and throw them out. Jane gripped the dash for stability. Every so often they would splash through red muddy puddles that would obliterate the view through the windshield. Windshield wipers would scrape across the glass but do little more than leave muddy streaks. Robbie was better off driving with his head out of the window, which he did for a few seconds before overhanging branches struck the side of the vehicle and forced him back inside.

The last few times they had made the trip, Jane had looked terrified. Now Robbie noticed she was calm and collected as the car bounced over a bump so fast the wheels left the ground. They thudded back to the track with a loud creak from the suspension. Robbie had done it on purpose. He glanced at Jane. She would normally be complaining by this point. Instead she was gazing thoughtfully through the window.

"Have you remembered anything more about what happened to you?" he asked with concern.

Jane shot him an annoyed look, which she quickly covered up. "I already said."

Robbie laughed. "I thought we'd got to the bottom of that Tarzan thing. You were in a fever, somebody looked after you. A tribe maybe? All that ape stuff was in your head."

"You weren't there," she said defensively and unconsciously rubbed the scar on her leg. Archie had removed the ant-head sutures, replacing them with wire stitches. He had admitted to Jane how impressed he was with the improvised stitching. "It was real."

They had been traveling for almost three hours, so Robbie thought there was no harm in voicing his motives for the trip. They didn't have enough fuel to return, so Jane would have to go to the town like it or not.

"Listen, Archie and me want you to see a doctor in the town."

Jane's expression was thunderous. "What?"

Robbie kept his tone reasonable. "There's one of those Doctors Without Borders posts there. You just need to get checked out properly."

"No!"

"Jane, it's just to be sure you're OK."

"And nobody consulted me about this? I might have an opinion on the matter?"

"You're sick and we're concerned—"

"God! You sound like the brother I don't have and don't want!" Robbie smarted from the comment. "I get Archie springing this on me, but you? I thought we were friends—but I guess I was very wrong about that."

Robbie had suffered enough arguments at home and always sought to avoid them, but Jane's contentious behavior irked him. "I risked my life looking for you! I was searching when no one else would! I got bit, chased, almost shot . . . at least you could have the courtesy of listening to me!"

The jeep hit a ditch and shuddered as the transmission struck rocks. Robbie cursed and hoped the vehicle wasn't damaged. The momentary distraction was enough to hush them both, until Jane spoke up in no more than a whisper.

"You don't believe me."

"Do you blame me? Some guy out there lives with the animals, talks to them, and looked after you despite attacking us? And then this eco-warrior just dumps you back in the camp, riding an elephant, and disappears into the forest." He risked removing one hand from the wheel to demonstrate a magic puff of smoke. He decided to take a different tack to get his point across. "You know you have to be careful what you eat out there. A lot of it is poisonous and some of it is hallucinogenic, makes you see wild stuff. Can't you see that it was all just a feverish dream?"

Jane remained silent and refused to look at him. Now Robbie felt guilty. Jane had been through the wringer and didn't deserve his sharp remarks. He glanced at her, the way she pouted, the way her hair partially hid her profile—it all reminded him of Sophie.

"Sorry," he muttered. He wasn't used to apologizing but Jane had a knack of wrapping him around her finger.

Jane broke her frosty gaze and nodded graciously. He caught her staring at him several times.

"What?" he asked.

"Why are you out here?"

Robbie felt uncomfortable. He had always tried to avoid telling Jane about his life.

"I had a sister, Sophie . . . who died. She was all the family I had left. When that happened I felt I had no reason to carry on. So I ran away."

Saying "sorry" seemed rather pointless, so Jane remained silent for several minutes. It was the first time Robbie had mentioned his sister and she wanted to know more.

"I've been thinking about why people are here," said Jane.

"Deep."

"I mean here in the Congo. Everybody has a story. Clark has always been looking for risky gambles, we're stuck here because we're broke and have too many loan sharks looking for us. And you . . . because your sister died."

Robbie nodded in agreement. He didn't understand what her question was. He caught her staring at him with a frown.

"What're you thinking?" he said.

Jane shook her head, but something was obviously on her mind. After a few minutes of contemplative thought she spoke up.

"Tell you what. I'll go see the doctor if it keeps you and Dad happy."

"Thanks." He shot her a warm smile. She had caved in quicker than he'd anticipated.

"And when you go shopping for supplies, I'm going to find that Internet connection and try and email a few friends."

"Deal." Robbie was glad she was finally going along with the plan, but couldn't shake the feeling Jane was not telling him everything.

. . .

The town of Sango was a large collection of dwellings and shops clustered on the bank of a meandering tributary that fed the Congo River. Although most locals were farmers, armed rangers used the town as a base to counter poaching activities. The town also had a lucrative black market dealing with valuable animal parts that could be smuggled out via road, river, or air.

The fertile hills around Sango had been cultivated for potato crops, and the town boasted an airfield—or rather a strip of flat dirt and a corrugated-iron shelter that served as the terminal. Power cables and telephone lines followed a lone tarmac road that led to civilization.

As Robbie and Jane entered, they were immediately hit by the smell of progress—overstressed sewers, gasoline fumes from numerous vehicles that were no longer roadworthy, a market square with stalls selling meat and fish that hung in the afternoon sun and were swarmed by flies. Scrawny dogs strayed through the streets, scattering chickens foraging amongst the piles of plastic waste. Somewhere a radio played tinny Congo rumba guitar tunes. Raised voices and laughter filled a bar with young and old people clutching cold beers as they sat on ancient furniture.

They located the Doctors Without Borders post and Jane was seen to immediately. The doctor, an elderly Australian woman, was impressed with the care Jane's wounds had received. She could find nothing wrong, but agreed that there was every possibility Jane had had a fever, and fetched some antibiotics. That satisfied Robbie and he whispered to Jane:

"See, told you this Tarzan was just a bizarre hallucination. You'll be OK."

Jane didn't reply. She accepted a bottle of antibiotics just in case there was a slight infection. Both she and Robbie were thankful the doctor didn't inquire why they were in the middle of the jungle—the doctor had been in many Third World countries and had learned it was best not to ask.

Robbie took Jane to a building with white paint flaking from its façade. The handwritten sign above claimed it supplied mobile phones and had an Internet connection. The phones were all old recycled ones, and Jane was surprised to see she could get a signal, although her phone refused to connect to the single provider that flashed up.

Robbie paid for her Internet use upfront and set about purchasing supplies. He hated this part of his job, as it involved haggling, and he was never very good at it. Mister David had laughed many a time when Robbie had paid over twenty times the going rate. Now he was spending Archie's money, he had to be careful. He took one final look at Jane and was satisfied to see her engrossed in the computer screen.

• • •

Jane impatiently drummed her fingers as the modem dialed the number and went through a long series of squawks and beeps.

Once she was online she did a search for the name Tarzan, ignoring the search engine's unhelpful suggestion: *Do you mean Tanzania? . . .* and drew zero responses.

A search for *jungle ghost* returned almost four million unhelpful hits. Research was going to be tougher than she thought. *Plane Crash Congo* found over four hundred thousand articles, but most of the ones she browsed were all new occurrences. She stared at the screen thoughtfully.

Plane Crash Greystoke.

A much smaller list of options was returned. Jane felt her pulse quicken as she clicked on a link and the headline appeared: *Lord and Lady Greystoke presumed dead.*

"Lord?" she said to herself—and the power to the connection took that opportunity to drop. She banged the mouse in frustration as the screen went blank and received a stern look from the young shopkeeper who was seated on the window ledge watching the boats in the port. "Sorry."

"It'll be up again in no time," assured the shopkeeper. No time turned into forty minutes. As soon as the computer bleeped back to life, Jane went through the aggravatingly long dial-up process and found the article again. This time she expanded it.

Controversial conservationist Lord John Clayton Greystoke and his wife, Lady Alice Greystoke, were officially declared dead today after an enquiry found they most likely perished in an airplane crash while on a scientific undertaking in the jungles of Zaire.

Jane scrolled through the article and found a photograph of the dashing Lord and Lady. The very same faces she had seen in the photograph recovered from the aircraft cargo hold. A shiver ran down her spine as she continued reading.

Most famous for their outspoken views on how world governments were ignoring environmental concerns and failing to support groups who were dedicated to preserving both the environment and endangered species, the Greystokes had spent a portion of their personal wealth to follow in the footsteps of great environmentalists such as Dian Fossey. Their travels around the globe, to protest the destruction of rainforests and demand government intervention, were often met with lackluster official support. The couple had planned an expedition into the Congo rainforest to gather scientific evidence of man's damage to the ecosystem, a venture the Foreign Office strongly warned against due to the intense fighting in the region. Their private jet vanished over east Zaire and no distress signal was detected. What brought the aircraft down remains a mystery. Earl Greystoke was said to be piloting at the time. Lady Greystoke is thought to be the only other victim lost. She was five months pregnant with their first child and had hoped to return to England for the birth . . .

Jane gasped and reread the sentence. Pregnant? Could it be that they survived the crash for four more months, at least until their baby was born? That was a huge assumption to make, but Tarzan's existence supported it. It also begged the question as to how they'd died.

Jane examined pictures of the Greystokes, which were clearer than the damp photo she had found, and now she was struck by their uncanny similarity to Tarzan. There was no doubt in Jane's mind. Even the dates of the crash tallied. Tarzan was their son.

She clicked through more articles, each one repeating the same information. A few touched on the fate of the Greystoke estate, but Jane was more interested in any references to their son. The only other news snippet was: *Greystokes confirm pregnancy rumors.* Then a name caught her eye: *D'Arnot.* She clicked on the link. It was from a more sensational newspaper:

The world was shocked last week when missing French UN Peace-keeper Paul D'Arnot staggered from the Congo jungle after being missing for almost eleven months following an insurgent attack on his unit.

D'Arnot claimed that a mysterious boy, who lived with a band of wild gorillas, had nursed him back to health. He further claimed to have proof that the boy was son of the missing Lord Greystoke, who had allegedly crashed in the forest eleven years earlier. The Greystoke estate dismissed the rumors as nonsense, saying D'Arnot's claims were nothing more than a confidence trick to get his hands on the Greystoke fortune. D'Arnot is set to undergo psychiatric evaluation.

So D'Arnot had reached civilization, only to be greeted with skepticism. Jane knew how he must have felt. So he had attempted to return to Tarzan, and that is what got him killed.

What should she do? Who could she contact to inform the world that she had found Lord Greystoke's heir? Why would she be believed any more than D'Arnot? People would assume she was just digging for the Greystoke fortune too. Then she reeled . . . that made Tarzan a lord! A very rich lord! A thousand questions rushed through her mind but she muted them all with one fact—she needed to tell Tarzan the news first. How would he react? Jane suspected that he wouldn't care.

"Jane?" Robbie stood at the door, a boxes cradled in his arms. "Ready to go in twenty minutes?"

Jane nodded, deliberately using her body to block his view of the monitor. "Great."

When she was sure Robbie had gone she turned back to the screen and continued skimming through articles. No more information seemed to be forthcoming. She was about to close the machine down when another thought hit her. Checking that Robbie wasn't around, she typed in: *Robbie Canler.*

The few results yielded nothing relevant. After a moment's thought she tried:

Robert Canler New York Missing Person.

She was surprised to find an exact match. She caught a few words: *Robert Canler—missing—sister found dead—wanted for murder.*

Then the town's power went down again and the words vanished.

14

With the jeep refueled and weighed down with supplies—mechanical parts, full fuel canisters, a new inflatable raft to enable Clark to guide the logs downstream, and enough rice to last for weeks—Robbie made careful progress back to Karibu Mji. They had spent longer than necessary as Jane had insisted on waiting until the power was restored so she could send an email. Robbie had agreed, pleased to see her mood had improved. Now it was approaching sunset, but the sky was already dark with brooding clouds as the heavens unleashed their payload.

Only one headlight worked on the jeep and Robbie was unable to find a spare. The jungle track was slick with mud and he had to concentrate on keeping the vehicle on the road, particularly when the steep track became nothing more than a raging stream as it flooded.

For four hours they drove through the storm, the path ahead occasionally illuminated by violent forks of lightning. They barely exchanged any words, and Robbie's shoulders were beginning to ache from the physical act of steering. Several times the jeep slipped in the quagmire and the tires freely spun like muddy pinwheels before reconnecting with the earth.

Just when Robbie was beginning to think they wouldn't be able to make it any further through the storm, the rain abated to a fine trickle. He suspected it was only temporary, but seized the opportunity to step heavily on the accelerator.

"How did your sister die?' asked Jane, picking up the thread of the conversation from hours earlier.

Robbie was instantly cautious. Jane had never asked questions before. He was never sure if it was due to lack of interest or politeness.

"I . . . I don't know," he admitted.

After months of wanting to speak to Jane about how he felt, he was suddenly struck mute. He coughed and gripped the wheel unnecessarily hard as they bounced along the track.

"She was abused, beaten by . . . by Graham, our stepfather." At first the words reluctantly came, but now he was talking rapidly, relieved to finally speak about it. "I think it was a blow on the head. She had a bump for a week from when he shoved her head against the wall. I thought it was nothing worse than he'd done before. We were always getting knocked around. But this . . . it didn't go. She complained that she felt light-headed. I should have acted then. Done something . . . took her to a doctor, but I'd started to sleep away from home. I was gone for a week—" images of that fateful day filled his thoughts. "One day I got back and she was dead. Our wonderful mother was passed out and Graham was in front of the TV. Watching a comedy show." He sneered at the memory, the rage he had felt resurfaced.

"And that's why you ran away?" Jane probed.

Robbie remained silent. He couldn't tell her the truth . . . could he? He had wanted to confess his sins in the vain hope that he would feel better and be released from the guilt he had been hoarding. He just couldn't bring himself to do it. Not here, not now. What would Jane think of him if she knew the terrible truth?

They were both tight-lipped until the rain picked up again and relentlessly drummed on the jeep's roof and obscured the windows. They had to be close to the camp, but Robbie could see no sign of it.

"You tried to kill him, didn't you?" said Jane suddenly.

Robbie was so shocked that the jeep almost veered off the road as he stared at her. Jane yelled, reaching over to correct his steering. The vehicle skidded back on track.

"Watch it!" snapped Jane.

"How do you know?" barked Robbie.

"I read about it on the Internet."

Jane didn't look at him. Robbie opened his mouth a few times to shout, to argue, to accuse her of spying . . . but a large part of him was glad his secret was out.

"I took a wrench from his toolbox. He was just sitting there with his back to me, laughing at the TV while Sophie lay dead." His voice was bitter, his lip curled in a snarl as he relived the emotions. "He didn't hear me coming. I just walked up and slugged him on the head." He winced, remembering the terrible crack his stepfather's skull had made, and the blood . . . so much blood.

"I just turned. Turned and ran." To his surprise Jane squeezed his arm in sympathy. "So . . . there you have it. That's why I ran. I'm a murderer."

The words were like lead in his mouth, but the moment they had escaped he felt a weight had shifted from his shoulders. He glanced at Jane, thinking it was odd that she hadn't recoiled in fear. Ahead, the perimeter lights of the encampment twinkled through the trees.

"We're back," he said, relieved they had spoken but thankful he could scurry off to find some solitude.

"You're wrong, you know," said Jane softly.

Robbie parked next to the bar. He killed the engine. "Wrong about what?"

Jane climbed from the jeep, keen to stretch her legs.

Robbie followed her out, confused as to why she was taking the news so well. "I don't get it. What am I wrong about?"

Jane shook her head and was about to reply—

Automatic gunfire sliced through the air and Robbie and Jane threw themselves to the ground. Bapoto stood on the bar's porch, an AK-47 pointed menacingly at them. His sickening grin made it clear the next shots wouldn't be warning ones.

Tafari stepped from the bar, smoking a cheap cigar and dressed in dirty military fatigues. Robbie caught a glimpse inside the building—

it had been trashed. Everybody was inside, on their knees, hands on their heads, Tafari's militia guarding them.

"You must be the daughter, *non?*" Jane looked defiantly at him. "Not one for conversation, eh? Well, you must think me rude. I am General Tafari, but you know that already, huh? Is that what you went to town for? To report where I am?"

"We went for food and supplies—" said Robbie before Bapoto whacked him across the cheek with the butt of his rifle.

Tafari shot his man an annoyed glance. "You are supposed to do that if he *doesn't* talk. Not shut him up!"

"He was telling the truth," said Jane. "We had to get supplies. We never said a word about you, why would we?"

Tafari scrutinized her and Jane stuck her chin defiantly out. "You have more courage than your father. He groveled for mercy."

Jane refused to be intimidated. She had stood her ground while being charged by a bull gorilla; in comparison Tafari was nothing.

"You're pathetic!"

Tafari laughed and wagged a finger at her. "I see I must watch you most carefully. It is unfortunate for you that you said nothing, ha-ha! Now we have no need to worry that the cavalry will be looking for you!" He leaned close and blew foul smoke at her. "Out here, the jungle will swallow you whole and spit you out. You will not be missed." He nodded to Bapoto. "Bring them out."

Bapoto nudged the bar door open and shouted to his men. The loggers were led out at gunpoint, their paths illuminated by the flashlights strapped to the soldiers' rifles.

Robbie winced when he saw that Archie, Clark, Esmée, and Mister David had been beaten. Clark appeared to have taken the brunt of it and his right eye was swollen shut. As soon as Archie saw Jane he motioned toward her.

"Have they hurt you?"

Bapoto punched Archie in the gut—Jane swung for the thug, but stopped when Oudry pointed a rifle at her face.

Esmée glanced at Robbie and Jane, her face glazed in terror, and Robbie guessed she was reliving the trauma she'd experienced during the war. Robbie counted only fifteen people, excluding himself and

Jane. Whether the missing men had fled or been murdered he couldn't guess. Bapoto ordered the prisoners to kneel in the mud and Robbie feared the worst—it was beginning to look like an execution. Tafari gripped him around the collar and booted him in the backside.

"Join them. You too," he said, shoving Jane.

Robbie refused to kneel but a guard delivered a swift rifle butt to the back of his legs to drop him. Jane knelt, scowling at her captors. All the captives looked miserable, rain soaking them. Tafari strutted, puffing cloying cigar smoke.

"Some would say I am a generous man. I gave you the right to cut my trees down. I gave you protection and what do you give me in return? You try to overthrow me!" Tafari's paranoia had grown during the forced march to the loggers' camp. With each step Tafari was increasingly convinced the Americans were using the logging as a pretext to overthrow him.

"I told you," croaked Archie through a split lip. "We thought you were sabotaging our equipment. Why would we do the same to you?"

"You continue with your lies! Should I cut your deceitful tongue out?" He pulled a knife from his belt. The blade was wicked and black. He yanked Archie's head back, squeezing his jaw open with one hand.

"NO!" screamed Jane. "It wasn't us! It was Tarzan. He's the *Negoogunogumbar!*"

Tafari immediately stopped and Jane reveled in the frightened expression on face. Evidently he was a superstitious man.

"She tells the truth," said Mister David. The guard nearest him raised his rifle to strike him silent, but stopped when Tafari gestured for him to continue. "The spirit has been hounding our men. Stealing and breaking equipment. This forest is cursed."

Jane caught Mister David's eye; did he believe her now?

The rebels exchanged uneasy looks. Murder and war was only fun when the dead didn't return for retribution. Tafari could see his men weaken and cut their jabbering with a sharp cry.

"Enough of this folklore! Tie them up." He whirled round to face Archie. "If this place is truly haunted then we will raze it to the ground."

The hands of the fifteen prisoners were tied with plastic cable ties that looped around the wrists and tightened painfully. Archie and

Clark watched in despair as Tafari organized his men to torch the camp. They used the extra fuel Robbie had brought back to feed the fire. Despite the driving rain, every building went up in magnificent orange flames.

Archie and Clark watched as their dreams for the future were destroyed. Then again, their hopes for even a short-term future were looking uncertain.

Tafari rounded his men up and they filed the prisoners from Karibu Mji as it burned down behind them.

• • •

The guerrillas had hiked for a day and a half, initially following the route Bapoto had taken around the base of the mountain so they could surprise the loggers. On an impulse, Tafari had diverted them over the uncharted mountain, a tactic that had gained them half a day. However, now the raid was over, they took the easier route back, following the dirt track that led to the valley, beyond which lay their barracks.

Robbie and Jane walked together, heads bowed against the rain. They were soaked to the skin.

"He bought that Tarzan line," muttered Robbie.

"Did you see his face? He knows it's true," said Jane with a smile. "I didn't hallucinate anything."

"Well, if your mysterious Tarzan was around why didn't he try to rescue us? I think we should start taking things into our own hands."

He checked nobody was watching. The Stygian darkness provided the perfect cover as he pulled out his pocketknife. With some difficulty he opened the blade.

"What are you doing?" hissed Jane as he sawed through her plastic restraint.

"Keep you hands together. Make it look like they're still tied. Now do mine."

Jane checked nobody was looking. The guerrillas kept to the flanks, heavy hoods pulled over their heads to shield them from the elements. Rain dripped from the weapon barrels poking from under their ponchos. They didn't pay any attention to their prisoners as Jane cut Robbie's cuffs.

From their position near the rear of the procession, Jane couldn't see how it was possible to pass the knife to any other logger. Her father, Clark, and Esmée were at the front, too far to get a whispered message to.

"What now?"

"We make a run for it as soon as we can."

Jane was aghast. "What about the others?"

"There's thirty-three rebels and seventeen of us," Robbie whispered grimly. "We better hope we can get away for help and they don't hurt the others."

"We can't just leave them!"

"If you have any better ideas let me know," said Robbie helplessly. Running was their only choice and it was a desperate one. He didn't harbor any doubts that Tafari would rather shoot them in the back of the head than let them escape.

Jane understood their situation was dire. This could be the last chance she had to speak to Robbie.

"Remember what I said earlier, about your sister?"

"Not now," hissed Robbie. "Eyes right, the ground slopes away."

Jane glanced across. In the light offered by a rebel's flashlight she could see the side of the track was a sharp incline into thick bush. A flicker of approaching lightning revealed that it was their best opportunity for escape.

"We go together. On three."

Robbie tensed, his heartbeat increased as he counted. Blood pounded in his ears and his own voice became indistinct. He just hoped Jane could hear him.

"Three!"

He shoved Jane off the trail and they both slid down the muddy incline. The darkness and rain gave them several seconds' lead before the nearest captor realized what the noise was.

"*Arrêtez!*" He fired blindly.

Robbie and Jane ran for their lives. Bullets whizzed around them, thunking into the ground or splintering wood in the darkness ahead. They had no illumination because storm clouds blocked the moon.

Branches slapped them in the face and roots and creepers tripped them as they ran. Jane grabbed Robbie's belt. If they were separated in the darkness they stood no chance.

The shouting behind them increased and gunfire cracked through the darkness. She prayed Tafari was not punishing the other prisoners for their actions. A quick look over her shoulder revealed a dozen flashlights bobbing in their direction. Then a clear voice rang out:

"I see them!"

Robbie dragged Jane sharply to one side as bullets shredded a tree next to them. Sharp splinters of wood struck his cheek. The ground suddenly gave way to water and Jane stumbled. For a second she feared they had run into a river—a fate that could deliver a quicker death than their pursuers. Lightning revealed they were in a stream. Robbie stepped up the pace as the flashlights kept in pursuit.

"Come on!" he shouted encouragingly, clambering up the bank.

His foot suddenly slid into a burrow. With a sickening crunch Robbie keeled over. White-hot pain seared through his leg.

Jane was several feet ahead before she realized Robbie had fallen. She raced back to him, as lightning rippled.

"What's wrong?"

"Think my ankle's broken!" he hissed in pain.

The flashlights were rapidly approaching, the voices getting louder. She tried to help him stand.

"On your feet!" she growled.

Movement just made the pain worse and Robbie crumpled. He pushed Jane away.

"Go! Get out of here!"

"I can't just leave you here!"

"Run!"

Jane's hesitation cost her dearly. The flashlights were suddenly veering toward them and weapons were armed with a cold click-clack. Robbie raised his hands.

"I surrender."

Bapoto pushed through his men and sneered when he saw Robbie's predicament. "Does it hurt?"

Robbie remained defiantly silent. Bapoto placed a chunky boot on Robbie's ankle and pressed. "What about now?"

Robbie screamed in pain—then suddenly spluttered into silence. Bapoto thought he had passed out, which was a shame because he had planned to inflict a lot more pain. But Robbie was staring upward, his mouth open in astonishment. Bapoto followed his gaze to the dark canopy.

For a split second, lightning silhouetted the muscular figure standing in the boughs above them.

"Tarzan!" yelled Jane in delight.

As they were plunged back into darkness, the two men either side of Bapoto were jerked into the air, their fingers scrabbling at the nooses around their necks. One man dropped his gun while the other kept his finger on the trigger as he was hoisted up.

The gun's strobing muzzle flashes made the unfolding events difficult to follow. The automatic's stray fire was capable of six hundred rounds per minute—and the choking man emptied a full clip, half of which raked into another rebel, killing him instantly.

Bapoto fired into the tree as everybody's flashlights convened to where they thought the mysterious figure was—but the bullets just chewed up an empty branch.

In the flashes of gunfire, Bapoto saw Jane look up—then she suddenly vanished between one strobing flash and another.

Robbie saw her disappear too, his doubts about Tarzan now replaced by hope. He hadn't managed to escape, but Jane had.

"Go!" he yelled. But he was shouting to empty space. Tarzan and Jane had disappeared into the night.

15

The gunfire and violence would once have had Jane sobbing and shaking, but she felt safe with Tarzan as he spirited her away in the night, leaping and swinging from the trees at breakneck speed. No matter how adept he was in the jungle he wasn't impervious to bullets and cold steel.

Tarzan kept close to the mountain as the storm intensified and they progressed ever upward. After some time, they stopped to rest on a rocky outcrop on the steep slopes. Jane sensed a shift in the darkness and lightning revealed they were sitting amongst the low storm clouds, in the heart of the storm. They pressed themselves against the rocks while Tarzan rested.

"Jane hurt?" he finally asked.

"No. I'm not hurt."

Tarzan roughly twisted her head, arms, and legs to check for any injuries. Satisfied there were none, he turned to his own. Jane was shocked to see a streak of blood across his hip from where a bullet had grazed him.

"You're bleeding!" she reached out to help him, but Tarzan turned away and began examining the bushes around him. He took great care to select a broad leaf, which he then crunched in his hands. Jane could smell a pungent aroma as Tarzan dabbed the leaf on the wound. When he was finally done, he stood and motioned it was time to go.

"Come," he commanded with his usual brevity.

"Where are we going?"

"Home." In the dim light, Jane caught a rare look of concern on Tarzan's face.

"My father's in trouble. My friends. We must go back for them."

Tarzan shook his head. "Many men with guns. Tarzan cannot fight."

Jane wanted to argue, but he had a point. Before she could think of anything to say, Tarzan continued.

"Soldiers have your friends. Soldiers came through Tarzan's land while Tarzan watch you."

Jane understood. She hadn't seen him, but Tarzan had been watching her every move at the camp, no doubt concerned since he didn't trust the loggers. It was fortunate he had done so or else Jane would never have escaped. She hoped Robbie hadn't been punished for his escape attempt. Esmée had told her many stories of the ruthless executions Tafari had performed on those who angered him.

"Thank you." The words sounded weak and failed to convey the true flood of gratitude Jane felt. Then she guessed why Tarzan looked so concerned.

"You think the soldiers may have found your home?"

Tarzan nodded, his face grave. Jane suddenly felt sick. Tafari was a barbarian toward his own race; what would he do to a band of defenseless gorillas that crossed his path? Reluctant at leaving her father and the others in Tafari's hands, she nodded and stood. Tarzan was no match for heavily armed soldiers; her only hope lay in Tarzan taking her back to civilization so she could raise the alarm.

Tarzan helped her on to his back, then leapt into the trees, bounding from trunks and branches with purpose. Jane closed her eyes and held tight—they were moving faster than ever before.

In the dead of night, as the storm raged around them, they crowned the mountain, heading toward Tarzan's home.

• • •

Robbie drifted back to consciousness with a ferocious headache. Even with his eyes open he saw little but inky blackness. Pain shot up his foot and he gasped for air.

"Try not to move," said a voice. It sounded vaguely familiar, but Robbie struggled to remember the name.

"Where are we?" It was little more than a croak. His mouth was dry, but his face was damp from rain.

"We stopped to rest. You're bleedin' lucky to be alive," whispered a voice that Robbie recognized as Clark's.

"Hold still," said the first voice, which he now identified as Archie's. His vision slowly swam into focus, and he realized he was lying on his back, with Clark sitting a couple of feet away with a stony expression. He was deliberately not making eye contact with Robbie, but he could see the concern on his face. Robbie tried to sit up, but he was pushed back down.

"I said don't move," hissed Archie's voice from near his feet. Robbie twisted his head and saw that Archie was tying Robbie's foot in an improvised splint made from two branches and secured with vines.

A quick look around revealed the other prisoners were all sitting forlornly in the muddy road, spread out to make communication between them difficult. The moon was now shining through the passing storm clouds and Robbie could see the rebels sitting under the trees lining the road, eating and laughing amongst themselves.

"Where's Jane?" Robbie croaked.

"I thought you could tell me," said Archie. "We heard gunfire."

"We ran . . ." He remembered their flight through the bush; his foot sinking into the burrow and his ankle snapping. "I tripped over. Told her to run . . . but she came back."

Archie had stopped binding his wound and was looking at him, devastated.

"It was a brave thing you tried," mumbled Clark.

Archie's head bobbed in agreement. "They said they shot her." His voice was little more than a hoarse whisper as emotion choked it.

Then Robbie's memories came flooding back and he sat bolt upright so fast the pain in his leg forced him back to the ground.

"Argh!"

"It's broken," said Archie plainly. "You're running a fever and we have nothing to combat it."

"Jane's OK," hissed Robbie as he recalled the phantom standing in the trees above them. "She's not dead."

Archie could scarcely believe it. "She got away?"

"He came. He came and saved her."

Archie frowned, wondering if Robbie was delirious.

"Who came?" he whispered, frightened of drawing their guards' attention.

"Tarzan," gasped Robbie as new pangs shot up his leg. "Tarzan. He's real. He's real . . ."

Archie and Clark exchanged grim looks. It looked like delirium was taking hold.

• • •

A pale mist cloaked the mountain as the sun rose. Visibility was just a matter of feet and it had forced Tarzan to the forest floor. Here at least Jane could keep pace with him.

They had walked for hours. Dull light struggled to pierce a thick mist that swallowed every noise. Jane was so focused on the ground in front of her that she almost walked into Tarzan. He had stopped in his tracks as the trees ended and the plateau clearing began.

Jane could see the dark aircraft hulk and immediately sensed something was wrong. A cry of grief from Tarzan drew her attention to two bodies on the floor. They sprinted across to a blackback and silverback that lay dead, their bodies riddled with bullets.

Tarzan wailed and Jane choked back tears. The aircraft was peppered with bullet holes and empty cans and plastic wrappers littered the plateau, signs that Tafari's men had stopped here on their way to the loggers.

Tarzan crouched beside the bodies, examining the wounds and making low grief-stricken grunts. The plateau felt abandoned and the stench of death lingered even in Jane's nostrils. Then she saw the burnt remains in the bonfire by the entrance to the aircraft. She gave a sharp intake of breath when she noticed a pair of severed gorilla hands and legs poking from the fire. Charred bones had been cast aside as the rebels had gorged on the bushmeat. Jane had heard that poachers considered it a delicacy, but she was staggered to believe people could bring themselves to eat gorillas' flesh. It was tantamount to cannibalism!

Violence flickered behind Tarzan's eyes as he gazed at the remains. Then he lifted his head to the sky and uttered a blood-curdling ululation while beating his chest. Jane stepped away when Tarzan began tearing at the ground, bounding on all fours, kicking the bonfire over, and pounding the hull of the aircraft. It reminded her of how Kerchak had behaved when she first arrived, but she had never seen Tarzan act with such rage.

Suddenly she became aware of movement in the mist. The gorillas were returning and Jane went tense with fear as Kerchak appeared at her side. He bore fresh scars, but looked as strong as ever. He glanced at Jane with distaste, but stood by her side and gave a low cough.

A dozen other gorillas timidly appeared, circling them. Jane heard the gallop of tiny feet and Karnath jumped into her arms, holding her tight. Jane was relieved that the young ape had avoided the rebels' senseless slaughter, and pressed the damp bundle of fur close to her cheek.

Tarzan stopped his display of grief and approached the group. They crowded around him, thankful to have one of their own safely back. Tarzan walked amongst them, touching their heads, checking who was missing.

He reached Kerchak and touched a gash on the gorilla's head. The great ape grunted in pain, but allowed Tarzan to examine him.

"Men did this," Tarzan stated with venom.

Jane gently took Tarzan's hand. "The people who did this are the same ones who have my family captive."

She doubted she could convince Tarzan how important it was to her that her family and friends were saved; after all, he still thought of them as his enemies.

Tarzan's eyes narrowed and Jane admonished herself for under-estimating him—it was clear he knew the difference.

"Tarzan will get revenge," he snarled.

Jane smiled encouragingly. "Yes! You need to take me to a city so we can get help. They can get the army involved and we can—"

"Revenge at Tarzan's hands!" he barked.

Jane hesitated. She needed to keep him on her side and didn't relish arguing with him.

"Tarzan, you can't. If you run into Tafari's camp he will kill you. You can't fight bullets!" Tarzan turned away, his mind was set. Jane sighed and lowered Karnath to the floor. She took Tarzan's arm and tried to twist him around—she would have better luck moving the aircraft. Instead she blocked his path. "Tarzan, no! It's suicide! You will be killed. Do you understand? One man can't fight those rebels!"

Tarzan stared at her. That one glance conveyed his intelligence and cunning. The corner of his mouth twitched in a bitter smile.

"Tarzan not one man. And Tarzan fears nothing!"

Then he stood on the edge of the cliff and bellowed his challenge to the world.

• • •

Clark couldn't identify the smell, but it was vaguely familiar. Archie recognized it immediately. It was the stench of death and decay. During his medical career he had been around enough corpses to recognize it in the room they had been locked in.

It was midday by the time they reached the rebels' camp and everybody's feet hurt from the exhausting forced march. Both Archie and Clark's backs were aching from carrying an unconscious Robbie between them.

Bapoto had been almost gleeful when he led his captives into the windowless hut at the edge of the rebel base. The tarnished iron door had swung noisily open; they were herded inside and shackled to the supporting wooden posts with thick, black chains. Bapoto had obviously done this many times before and each captive wondered about the fate of the previous prisoners. Unfortunately the signs were all around them in the dark stains on the walls.

Robbie only came around an hour after Bapoto had imprisoned them. The air was thick and humid and sweat clung to his brow.

"Where are we?"

Archie looked up from his position near a small crack in the wall, one of many ill-fitting panels that allowed shafts of light to seep in.

"In Tafari's hellhole."

Clark was slumped in the corner, unconscious. Robbie nodded to him.

"Is Clark OK?"

"They hit him because he wasn't walking fast enough." Archie redirected his brooding gaze to the crack, then added as an afterthought, "How are you feeling?"

"Can't feel my foot."

"I braced it best I could. Count yourself lucky that your fever's gone."

Robbie tried to stand, but staggered as his foot gave way. He supported his weight on a post the second time and managed to stand. He hobbled over to Clark but was pulled short by the chain around his good leg.

"We've got to get out of here," said Robbie firmly.

Esmée looked up. He hadn't noticed her curled against a post, nursing her head in her hands. "It won't happen, Robert. This is Tafari's death camp. People don't walk away."

Robbie felt sick and looked around. Most of the loggers were slumped on the floor, a few asleep. Serge avoided eye contact. Mister David had taken a severe beating and looked vacantly into space.

"What do they want from us?" demanded Robbie.

"Tafari sees us as a threat," Archie replied, savoring a sweet-scented waft of air that drifted in from the jungle. "He thinks we've been sabotaging his camp in a plot to overthrow him."

"That's ridiculous! We haven't done anything! It was Tarzan."

Archie glanced at Robbie and shook his head. "You must have hit your head harder than I thought."

"I'm not imagining it. It's true. Jane told me how he'd been trying to scare everybody from the jungle."

"Tarzan? *Negoogunogumbar?*"

Even though he had saved Jane, Robbie felt anger toward the mysterious Tarzan. He was responsible for all this mess.

"He's real. I saw him."

"You don't know what you saw," said Archie dejectedly. "It was dark. Confusing."

"I saw him! He saved Jane."

"Jane's dead," spat Archie, his hope extinguished. "They told me. I heard the shots. Jane's dead and soon, so are we."

Archie peered out of the crack again. Robbie was furious. He looked around the room and noticed everybody wore the same expression: defeat.

"This is not over!" snapped Robbie. He tugged his chains. "We can get out of here—and Jane's not dead! I saw her taken right in front of me!" The chain didn't give and Robbie knelt down to examine the lock. It was old and took a single key. He rooted in his pocket for the knife, but it must have fallen out.

A blast of fresher air swept into the room as Bapoto opened the door and stepped in, his kukri in one hand.

"General Tafari wants to speak to you." He jabbed the kukri toward Archie and Robbie. "You, you—up." Archie reluctantly stood, as did Robbie. Bapoto rounded on him. "Ah, the cripple walks again, eh?" The thug pressed the blade against Robbie's cheek. "And don't think I've forgotten you."

Bapoto sniggered and pulled a single key from his belt and unlocked both Robbie and Archie. He didn't seem concerned about them running away. In fact, they were so weak and tired they could barely walk. Robbie was forced to use Archie as a crutch.

Bapoto slid a heavy wooden spar across the metal door to lock it, then shoved Archie toward the main buildings. Robbie tried to notice everything around him. The camp was twice the size of Karibu Mji and had been on the same location for some time. Their prison stood on the west side, away from the main complex. Opposite, fuel drums were stacked next to the gasoline generator. The main buildings sat to the north of the clearing and consisted of fourteen lodges standing at the side of a river. The largest looked to be a barracks with many opened windows covered with mosquito netting. A large mess pavilion had no walls, just a roof to protect it from the sun and rain. Robbie guessed the other buildings were a kitchen and various storage sheds. A single wooden guard tower stood at the edge of the clearing, a machine gun bolted to the platform above. A truck and four jeeps were parked behind the barracks in a small area that served as a parking lot and had a single dirt track leading out. There was no fence; evidently Tafari was not concerned about his prisoners escaping. With the thick jungle around them, he didn't need to worry.

Two large dogs were tied to a post, slumbering in the afternoon sun. One growled and pricked its ears when they passed. Robbie couldn't help but notice the scattering of bones around the animals. Bapoto led them to a large picturesque cabin that looked completely out of place. Robbie thought it resembled a vacation home.

Tafari sat on the porch in a rocking chair, smoking his usual vile cigar. Through the windows behind, Robbie saw walls bedecked with stuffed animal heads. A pair of gorillas and several chimpanzees stood out from amongst the big cats.

"You vex me," said Tafari standing as they approached. He tapped his head. "I have been thinking of why you would bite the king of the jungle—the hand that feeds you. It is impossible to overthrow me."

"How many times does it take to get through to your fat head? We thought *you* were attacking *us*," snarled Archie. Impending death had done wonders to improve his confidence, and imagining Jane dead somewhere in the jungle fueled his anger. "I came to complain and all you did was drive your percentages up like the petty crook you are."

Tafari stepped from the porch and flashed his perfect white teeth. "I remember you came to scout my village. Maybe see if we had weaknesses?"

Now Robbie saw the paranoid gleam in Tafari's eyes. "Tarzan is the one you want. You know he's out there, the jungle spirit, White Ape, whatever—call him what you want." Robbie jerked a thumb at Bapoto. "This goon saw him!"

Robbie felt a sharp blow hit his ear. It came from Bapoto.

"I saw nothing!" snarled the big man. "The girl snatched a gun and killed three men before we shot her."

Robbie was incredulous; Bapoto was covering up the truth to protect himself from his boss's wrath. Robbie suspected Tafari wouldn't hesitate inflicting a punishment on his second-in-command for such a terrible blunder. Robbie hoped he could use that to his advantage.

He pleaded with Tafari. "He's lying! Tarzan rescued Jane and killed your men. Do you really think a young girl could overpower one of you guys and then shoot three people?" He saw a flicker of doubt cross Tafari's face. He tried to capitalize on it. "Tarzan is the problem, General. Not us. Jane is still alive and with him. We make a good income together, why would we jeopardize that? If we work together—"

Bapoto grabbed Robbie around the scruff of his neck and shook him violently. Robbie's leg gave out and he floundered into the brute, almost tripping him.

"Enough!" snapped Tafari, raising a hand. He studied Archie and then grabbed his jaw and twisted him to face Robbie. "You see this face is a man grieving for the loss of his daughter. A loss you caused trying to escape. This is not a face that believes in your Tarzan. And if he don't believe it, why should I?"

Tafari gestured for Bapoto to make Robbie stand. Bapoto twisted Robbie's hands behind his back and forced him upright. Tafari ripped Robbie's shirt open, revealing his chest, and blew smoke into his face.

"I have ways of getting the truth out of people." Tafari's voice was smooth and casual. He took the cigar out of his mouth and held it close to Robbie's chest. Robbie flinched as he felt the intense heat. Tafari smiled amiably. "So, let us talk the truth."

• • •

There had been scarcely time to rest as Tarzan spoke to Kerchak. Jane knew "speak" was not strictly correct but she remained fascinated by the way they were able to grunt and bark in what seemed like communication. She sat away from the massacre and plucked green shoots from the farthest branches she could reach to feed Karnath, who stayed close by her side. In turn, the little ape darted up the tallest trees and returned with fruits that Jane gratefully ate.

Despite the urgency of the situation, she wanted to tell Tarzan what she had discovered about his past, but the ape-man didn't give her a chance. She retrieved the photo frame from the aircraft, removing the picture so she could fold it in her pocket.

Tarzan beckoned her over as the heavy mist parted and they were suddenly away to the trees with speed and purpose. She was now so used to their unusual mode of travel that she quickly realized they were traveling in a direction she had not been before.

Tarzan's pace was unforgiving, but even he was forced to the ground to rest and drink from the river. Jane watched as he bent low into the water and sipped. She cupped the clear liquid in her hands, most of which dribbled out by the time it reached her lips. It was cool and refreshing.

"Where are we going?" she finally had the chance to ask, hoping to hear the name of a familiar city.

"Numa."

Jane frowned. "I don't know what that means. We need to save my father and time is running out!"

"Numa will help."

"How?" Jane was feeling frustrated and didn't see any logic to Tarzan's plan. "Isn't family important to you? Don't you ever wonder who your parents were?"

"Tarzan's mother was Kala."

"No, she wasn't!" Tarzan looked surprised. Jane unfolded the picture and showed it to him. "These are your parents! That's your mother. They were on that plane when it crashed. They must have survived out here till after you were born. Do you remember any of that?"

Tarzan's brow furrowed as he processed the information. Jane knew he was intelligent, but had no idea how much of what she was saying was understood.

"Your parents were Lord and Lady Greystoke, from England. You are a lord, a very rich lord." She hadn't searched for articles about the current Greystoke's estate and the realization that this savage demon was in fact a posh English nobleman made her laugh. "You have a family, a *human* family who think you are dead. Doesn't that mean anything to you? My father is my only family. Robbie is my only friend here, besides you."

She slouched, tired of rambling. She was surprised when Tarzan lifted her chin and spoke softly. "Numa will help."

They were soon moving again, descending the opposite side of the mountain at great speed. Rainforest slowly transformed into a less dense forest. During their descent, Jane glimpsed a vast grassland through the trees, hemmed in by jungle-clad mountains. That was their destination.

Tarzan finally stopped on a rocky outcrop that poked over the forest as it petered out to dense grass that stood as high as Jane's shoulders. The view was magical. Fine motes caught in the morning sun and the grass swayed in waves as the gentle breeze caught it. Tarzan let Jane down, then bellowed a challenge.

His voice echoed across the valley.

Jane heard a familiar roar. She watched the grass sway as an animal approached. What she had presumed was one beast suddenly split into three as they spread out on their approach. Jane kept her nerve but was thankful Tarzan stood between her and the lionesses that emerged from the buffalo grass. The lead cat was unmistakable and Jane would have recognized her without the nick in her ear. It was Sabor.

Sabor snarled when she sighted her enemy. The other cats fanned out, and Jane noticed one was limping. They were the same pride that had attacked the gorillas. Why on earth was Tarzan bringing them here?

Tarzan leapt from the rock—and landed squarely in front of Sabor. He snarled a challenge and Sabor shrank back, ears flattened and tail quivering. It was clear who was master. Tarzan cocked his head to indicate that Jane should join him. Her legs trembled as she stepped down amongst the same predators that had been trying to eat her just a few nights earlier.

She kept close to Tarzan as he confidently strode through the grass. He was following Sabor, the limping lioness behind and the other at their flank. It occurred to Jane that the felines had them surrounded, though they made no move to attack.

Jane wanted to ask a hundred questions but knew the futility of seeking answers from Tarzan. Whatever power he held over these beasts, they begrudgingly respected him.

Parting grass revealed yet more grass ahead and Jane was becoming disoriented. They walked for several minutes before the long grass finally gave way and they stepped into a large clearing. Jane pressed closer to Tarzan, more terrified than she had ever been in her life.

Over a dozen lions lay on a large polished boulder, basking in the morning sun. Many were females, but Jane saw the shaggy dark manes of male lions that were rolling on their backs, paws in the air like common household cats. Jane would have considered the image cute if not for the dead wildebeest they had been feasting on. Most of the gnu had been devoured and was little more than bones with flies buzzing around them. Vultures sat at the edge of the clearing, waiting for their chance to feast. The lions' muzzles and paws were stained red, which gave them a grisly look. All eyes were fixed on the humans.

Sitting at the top of the boulder was a male lion, almost twice as big as the others. Its mane was voluminous and tinged with dark brown streaks. Its body and face were heavily scarred, medals of battles won. Its huge paws were stretched out and it yawned lazily, then sat to attention when it saw Tarzan. Jane knew without a shadow of a doubt that this was Numa.

A deep rumble built in the beast's throat. It was so bass-heavy that Jane could feel her ribs shaking. She dreaded to think what this behemoth thought of the two snacks that had dared enter its domain. Surely Tarzan wasn't thinking of fighting it?

Numa leapt from the boulder with a mighty thud and slowly approached them. Tarzan didn't move and Jane was convinced she was unable to. There was no way she could outrun a pride of lions.

The big cat paced closer . . . then, to her utter astonishment, Numa rubbed his great head against Tarzan's side and issued a guttural purr. Tarzan scratched the cat's head as if they were old friends.

Tarzan looked at Jane with a smile and she felt hope swell.

"Numa will help," assured Tarzan.

16

Darkness had fallen and Robbie hadn't stirred since they had been thrown back into the prison hut. Archie had pleaded for Tafari not to hurt them, but that had only resulted in a sadistic beating from the thug. Archie's hand was now swollen and he suspected he had several broken bones, but he had still fared better than Robbie.

All the prisoners were weak and hungry although Tafari had supplied water. He evidently planned to keep them alive a little while longer. With their shackles inhibiting movement, only Esmée could get close to Robbie. She was shocked at the ugly burns Tafari had inflicted. Robbie's broken ankle had also been pummeled as a torture.

"They are evil, evil men," she cursed as she bathed Robbie's forehead with the last of her water. The only illumination came from slivers of moonlight cast through gaps in the crooked wall panels.

"He's mad," said Archie. "Convinced we were planning to overthrow him."

"Do we look like insurgents?" croaked Clark. He had gained consciousness only to hear Robbie howling from the pains of his torture. His leg was bleeding from the numerous times he had tried to break his shackle to reach Robbie.

"To him we do," Archie croaked back.

No one else spoke a word, there was little point. The sound of Tafari's men laughing and joking drifted in as the guerrillas ate their evening meal. Static-laced music played from a radio.

What a new life they could have had, thought Archie. In three years he could have earned a lifetime's salary compared with back home. It was a big commitment in such an unpleasant environment, but he had always assumed that he would have plenty of time to convince Jane of the long-term benefits. He had been determined that she should not struggle later on in life. He sighed deeply and his ribs hurt; he suspected two of them must have broken under Tafari's mindless abuse.

Thinking about Jane hurt him to the core. There were many things he would have done differently, but the past was irreversible. He must be a terrible father for bringing her out here, and he didn't blame her for hating him. He hated himself.

He glanced over at Robbie, wondering why he had insisted Jane was still alive right until Bapoto and Tafari had beaten him senseless. Was he right? Archie didn't know how it was possible . . . unless she had been telling the truth about her jungle savior?

A faint glimmer of hope had cast his doubts away. He might die here, but the thought that Jane was still alive made him smile. He only hoped that, if it were true, she was running in the opposite direction as fast as she could.

• • •

Tafari tore a leg from the roasted jungle fowl on his plate. The jungle provided more than enough to feed his men and the table was filled with bushmeat. The camp's cook had done sterling work, but Tafari longed for another taste of the succulent gorilla flesh he'd experienced two nights previously. He counted himself fortunate to have found the band and felt satisfied in killing those too slow to flee. His brother, Samson, had been hunting in that region when he went missing, and Tafari wondered if it was the same band of apes responsible for his death. He was a superstitious man who preferred to believe the apes ate human flesh, rather than believe the so-called scientists who claimed gorillas were vegetarians.

His entire army was gathered under the pavilion, talking loudly as they recovered from the previous few days' hike. Beer was flowing and dozens of empty bottles had already been tossed to the floor. Keeping his men happy during good times and instilling fear in them when things turned bad was the key to Tafari's success.

He eyed Bapoto warily. His lieutenant was joking with Oudry next to him and, from his actions, was telling him how they had tortured their two prisoners. The fact the younger one had insisted the girl was alive had bothered Tafari more than he liked to admit. People usually broke and told the truth under the torture he administered, but his story had remained consistent, and that was a worry. It meant Bapoto was lying about executing her and had managed to convince his men to keep the truth from their leader.

Paranoia gnawed at Tafari. Was his lieutenant plotting a coup? His eyes darted across his men. How many of them were involved? His gaze set on Oudry, that lout who was always trying to impress Bapoto.

At that moment the generator failed and the lights went out. It was such a regular occurrence that the men cheered. At least they could still eat under moonlight and the battery-powered radio continued playing.

The mechanic responsible for maintaining the generator bolted from his seat to fix it. He had faced Tafari's belt in the past for letting it run out of fuel.

Tafari felt uncomfortable. He slipped a hand under the table and rested it on the reassuringly cold hilt of his sidearm. His eyes swept his men—none seemed ready to attack him. He relaxed a little, then noticed the dogs. They stood at the end of their tethers, both looking into the jungle with their ears rect. What had they sensed?

• • •

The mechanic reached the generator. It ran from an old truck engine he had ingeniously patched together. He was baffled, because he had made sure the fuel tank was topped up that very afternoon. He found the wind-up flashlight in its usual place near the fuel barrels and rapidly wound the dynamo. The light came to life and he cast it over the generator. The problem was immediately obvious—the flywheel belt had severed.

He took a closer step, his feet splashing through something wet. He shone the flashlight down to see the fuel cables had been yanked from the drums and gasoline was pouring out. He opened his mouth to raise the alarm—but a powerful hand clamped around his head and he was yanked backward into the undergrowth.

• • •

Tafari picked up his beer and strode across to the corner of the pavilion. He leaned on the wooden post and lit up a cigar, carelessly throwing the match to the floor. He took a swig of beer—then paused. Where had the engineer gone? He glanced at the dogs. They still stood to attention but hadn't barked. Tafari walked over to the dogs and scratched one between the ears.

"What do you see?"

He unfastened both their chains, expecting them to race away barking. Instead they held their ground. Ears twitched . . . then they began to whine. Their tails folded between their legs and they bolted amongst the buildings. Tafari was astonished. He had trained the dogs to be ruthless and had set them on to the occasional pygmy they found in the jungle. They had even chased a leopard from a tree—nothing scared them!

Tafari threw his beer down and unholstered his pistol. He ran back to his men and spoke in a hushed voice.

"We're under attack!"

The men didn't hear him and continued eating. Tafari's suspicious eyes darted around the moonlit base. He didn't want to cause a panic. He grabbed the radio and threw it against the nearest table, halting the music. Conversations spluttered and all eyes turned to him.

"We're being raided," he hissed.

The men exchanged glances. They knew from experience that ambushes tended to involve lots of gunfire and chaos. The camp was silent.

"Who?" said Bapoto looking around, a chunk of meat still in hand.

Tafari scowled at him and considered shooting him there and then to nip any pending coup in the bud—but he needed every man right now.

"The dogs have gone! The mechanic—where is he?"

This stirred the men and they looked around in alarm. Bapoto was the first out of his seat, snatching his rifle from where he had propped it against the table. The other men were less prepared; most had left their weapons in the barracks.

"Arm up!" hissed Tafari.

The men sprang into action, most rushing for the barracks—where they found the truck had mysteriously been pushed firmly against the door and its tires slashed. Tafari's temper exploded when Oudry returned to inform him that the men were having trouble rolling the truck away.

"How can this happen right under our noses?" demanded Tafari.

Bapoto looked uneasy. He was beginning to sweat, not from the humid jungle heat, but from fear. "The White Ape," he muttered.

Tafari glared at his lieutenant. "Which doesn't exist, does it? You have never seen it."

Bapoto looked away. Tafari's wrath would be worse than anything a supernatural spirit could administer.

• • •

"Something's happening," said Archie as he peered through a crack in the wall. "They're arguing. Running for their weapons."

The news had alerted everybody and they strained to overhear anything that would explain the rebels' panic.

Robbie suddenly coughed and Esmée gently lifted him upright. "Easy, my boy."

Robbie looked around. "How long was I out?" he winced. His entire body ached.

"A good few hours. Best thing to forget the pain."

"They're spreading out," reported Archie. "They're looking for something."

Robbie craned to see, gritting his teeth from the intense pain. "What's happening?"

"Seems they got wind of something they don't like. It's probably just a leopard scaring them."

Robbie doubted that. He knew exactly what it was.

"Tafari's heading this way!" Archie warned.

• • •

Jane crouched in a tree that afforded a clear view over the camp. The moon offered enough light to see the guerrillas racing across the camp. She was reminded of ants scurrying to protect their nest. She watched Tafari as he led a knot of men to a large building at the edge of the camp. He opened the door and peered in, appearing to speak to somebody. With the distance and light, Jane couldn't see inside the hut, but from the way the general secured the heavy wooden spar back in place she was certain she had pinpointed the prisoners. Exactly as she'd hoped.

With a faint rustle of leaves, Tarzan sprang up into the tree and stood next to her. Jane pointed to the prison hut.

"My father and the others are in that building. I'm going to have to get inside, they may be tied up."

Jane had expected a tirade of gallant refusals—no, it would be too dangerous, that's no job for a girl—the usual platitudes. Instead Tarzan simply nodded in agreement.

"Tarzan distract them."

Jane couldn't stop a smile from crossing her face. She was feeling strong and alert, driven by the desire to save her father and friends. With Tarzan at her side, it was just about possible.

• • •

Tafari ordered his men to spread out. He was confused—why hadn't they been attacked yet? Why the mischievous pranks? The very same stunts he had accused the Americans of performing.

In his consternation he started to believe the tales of the jungle spirit were true. How do you kill an angry forest ghost?

Gunfire came from the north. Tafari sprinted across as seven of his men emptied their automatic rifles into the trees. Tafari could see no sign of their target but joined them in firing blindly in the hope of hitting their aggressor. Branches were shredded under the bombardment and within seconds their ammunitions clips ran dry.

Then the forest exploded with activity. Several black giants barreled through the trees. Tafari couldn't see clearly enough but heard ferocious roars and saw three men plucked into the undergrowth, their terrified screams ending abruptly seconds later.

Out of ammo, the soldiers shrieked and retreated. Tafari cravenly pushed his men aside in the bid to be the first to safety. More gunfire erupted from the east side. A stray bullet must have caught the leaking gasoline because the fuel dump suddenly exploded with a deafening boom. A fiery mushroom cloud punched the sky and flames caught neighboring huts.

Tafari dropped to his knees and, with shaking hands, reloaded his pistol. He didn't know what was happening, but he had caught sight of terrible fangs when the jungle snatched his men. He swore he'd seen the face of the devil himself.

· · ·

Jane crept through the shadows behind the prison hut. Walking around to the main door would mean revealing herself to the rebels, and it would only take one bullet to stop her. She prodded the hut's walls. They were made from solid timber and immune to any punishment she could dole out. Luckily she wasn't alone.

· · ·

Mister David was the first to react to the loud thump against the rear wall. The planks buckled as they were struck again. Everybody else was pulling at their chains to try and peer through cracks so they could watch the drama unfolding outside.

Mister David and Serge scrambled aside as a third thud cracked the wood. All eyes turned fearfully as the pounding increased until a gaping hole was torn into the wall.

Esmée crossed herself and Mister David mumbled a prayer as a dark shape entered the prison. It was a huge silverback ape walking on its knuckles. It snorted at the prisoners, studying each in turn. A wave of fresh terror washed over the captives as the giant walked right in amongst them. Serge grasped his chain as the only defense from the wild animal . . . then a flash of blonde hair stopped him in his tracks.

Jane pushed past Kerchak and spotted her father. She ran over and hugged him.

"You're alive . . ." was all he could manage as tears rolled down his face.

More gunfire sounded from outside. The rebels had reloaded. Kerchak grunted, task complete, then quickly exited. Jane looked at the frightened faces.

"Where's Robbie?"

Robbie sat up and Jane ran over and hugged him tightly. "I thought they would kill you!"

"They gave it a damn good try," said Robbie between the jolts of pain from Jane's embrace.

"We've got to get you out." She examined the shackle around Robbie's leg and tried to pry it apart.

"No luck," lamented Esmée, suddenly seeing the chance of escape fizzle. Even the gorilla couldn't tear the steel clamps from their legs. "You need a key."

"Like this?" Robbie produced Bapoto's key from his pocket.

Archie gawped. The evening was turning into one big miracle. "How did you get that?"

Robbie grinned despite the pain across his bruised face. "All I had to do was get Tafari to hit me hard enough so I would fall against Bapoto. Then I snagged it from his belt."

"You took that beating just to steal a key?" said Archie incredulously.

Robbie shrugged. "It was the only plan I had. Besides, I knew Jane would come for us."

All eyes swiveled to Jane as she snatched the key and unlocked Robbie's shackles.

"Who you here with?" asked Clark, galvanized by the possibility of escape.

Jane grinned. "Tarzan. And he's brought a few friends."

• • •

Tafari was overseeing his men as they rearmed. He rummaged through crates of munitions, taking several hand grenades and clipping them to his bandolier. He selected a rocket launcher and slung it over his shoulder. He was a one-man army.

Outside was chaos. Soldiers were blindly shooting into the trees, wasting their precious ammunition. The fuel fire had ignited several buildings and small groups of men attempted to extinguish them with buckets filled from the river.

Bapoto ran to his leader's side. "They see nothing!"

"They're wasting bullets," snapped Tafari. He shoved Bapoto in the chest. "Get in the tower and cover the area!"

Bapoto ran to the watchtower and clambered up the rickety ladder to the gun nested above.

Tafari scrambled to put a plan together. Was this an attack on him or a rescue attempt? He glanced at the prison hut. The flames helped illuminate the area and he could see the door was still bolted shut. He began to rally his men.

"Don't shoot unless you can see your target!"

His men began to calm and form tight groups. Tafari hadn't maintained his position without developing strong leadership skills and by training his men hard every day. It only took a few moments for him to spread his troops around the camp, strategically hunkering down behind equipment and barrels, guns trained on the dark trees.

Bapoto took his position in the watchtower. He removed the safety catch from the high-caliber gun and swiveled it on its tripod mount a few times to ease the bearings. Then he peered into the darkness for any signs of the enemy, his finger hovering over the trigger.

The only sound that could be heard came from the chain of men darting between the river and the burning buildings.

Tafari took cover behind several empty fuel drums and scanned the darkness. Was it over?

Then he became aware of an unusual movement: Unless his eyes were deceiving him, the dirt on top of the barrels was vibrating. He

ANDY BRIGGS

looked closely. It was no illusion. He gently touched the barrel and felt the tiny vibrations. Then he placed an ear to the drum—the metallic cylinder amplified a sound.

The sound of approaching thunder.

Every soldier began noticing the ground tremble. From his lofty perch, Bapoto felt the tower sway and creak alarmingly. The rumble gained intensity and appeared to be coming from every direction.

Tafari stood, desperate to pinpoint the source of the noise. It was all around them.

With a violent crack the trees suddenly splintered apart. Several slender trunks toppled over, smashing through the center of the huts on the camp's periphery. They were followed by a herd of rampaging elephants emerging from the darkness.

Soldiers swiveled their weapons—but the first line of men were trampled underfoot as the elephants thundered into the encampment.

At their head was Tantor, slamming his bulk into buildings. Wooden frames creaked and toppled over, trapping men underneath. Bullets cracked and Tantor felt cold stings of pain, but that was not enough to stop him.

Before most of the soldiers could react to the assault, an unnerving roar came from behind.

Dozens of lions emerged from the trees at full speed. Three men were mauled before they could shoot. Tafari opened fire, gunning one of the lionesses down before he stopped, frozen in terror—

Numa stalked into the camp, Tarzan riding on his back. The terrifying vision made several rebels throw down their weapons and run for the trees—where Terkoz the gorilla and his band were waiting for them.

Numa's huge paws slashed the men foolish enough not to flee, while Tarzan swung his lasso—deftly looping it around a rifle and plucking it from a rebel's hand—leaving him open to Sabor's lethal jaws.

From the watchtower, Bapoto opened fire. The large-caliber machine gun shook the tower as it spat lead. Bullet casings whizzed past his ear and clattered to the floor. He had Tarzan in his sights.

Numa leapt over the bonnet of a jeep—landing on Oudry, who was hiding behind it. Tarzan gripped the beast's mane with one hand to keep his balance. He didn't flinch as Numa slashed mercilessly at Oudry. Bullets suddenly raked across the jeep, shattering the windshield. Tarzan flattened himself against Numa's flank and yelled a word of encouragement. The lion careered across the camp, zigzagging to avoid Bapoto's gunfire. Tarzan clung on to his mount, his eyes fixed on his quarry.

Bapoto couldn't swivel the gun fast enough to track the lion as it evaded his fire. The beast was heading straight for the tower, but he felt safe in the knowledge the lion wouldn't be able to reach him.

Numa shot past the tower and Bapoto momentarily lost sight of him. When he finally found his target again he was alarmed to see the White Ape was no longer on his back. With a sudden sense of dread, Bapoto leaned over the platform's handrail and saw Tarzan heading toward him with the agility of a monkey. The wild man bounded between the support posts and flipped on to the platform. Bapoto tried to swing the gun around but there wasn't enough room. Tarzan swiped the gun barrel with such ferocity that Bapoto lost his grip and the weapon pivoted around and struck him across the face.

Bapoto sprawled across the platform, dangerously close to falling over the side. Tarzan sprang for him as Bapoto drew his wicked kukri and plunged it toward Tarzan's heart. Tarzan gripped the guerrilla's wrist and they wrestled, Tarzan slowly inching the blade away from his chest. Bapoto was bigger than Tarzan, but because he was lying flat on his back, he couldn't use his weight.

With a desperate lunge, he twisted around and managed to throw Tarzan off. He jumped to his feet, knife at the ready—but he wasn't expecting Tarzan to use his powerful arms as a springboard to kick him in the ribs like a wild horse. The thug heard his ribs crack as he was sent teetering over the edge of the tower. His fingers scraped the handrail and he reached out for Tarzan for help. Tarzan offered none and Bapoto plummeted to his death.

• • •

From across the camp, Tafari saw his lieutenant fall—but his attention was dragged back to the battle where his men were falling under the lions' claws or being trampled by the elephants systematically bull-dozing the remaining buildings. He watched with anger as his own home collapsed when three elephants shoved it over, and as they then trampled the macabre trophies of death contained within.

To add to the chaos, Tafari now realized, gorillas were hiding in the trees, picking off fleeing rebels. How Tarzan had united the animals was a mystery, but Tafari was under no illusion he was losing the battle.

With a bellow that cut through the fight, Tarzan called out from the watchtower. His gaze was firmly on Tafari—but the general had the advantage. He pulled the rocket launcher from his shoulder and extended the tube. The missile was already loaded—all Tafari had to do was point and fire. He lined Tarzan up in the sights and pulled the trigger. He couldn't miss.

The missile shot across the clearing faster than Tarzan could move. Tafari had expected a perfect shot—but to his dismay the projectile arced away from his target as the heat-seeking sensors locked on to fires around the camp.

The missile curved toward the tower's base and prematurely exploded as it struck the supporting legs. The tower groaned and top-pled forward with Tarzan riding it the whole way down.

The tower smashed across the dining pavilion and Tarzan was thrown off as the platform splintered into a blazing building, scatter-ing lions and elephants from its path. The impact would have killed a man.

But not Tarzan.

For him, riding the toppling tower was no different from leaping through the trees. He hopped from the platform as it tore through the inferno and rolled through the flames so fast that he wasn't burned.

Tafari watched dumbfounded as Tarzan vaulted from the inferno and landed squarely in front of him. His eyes reflected the flames; he was covered in blood and grime—this was enough to convince Tafari that he was dealing with a malevolent inhuman creature.

Tarzan advanced upon him, clearly intending to tear him apart with his bare hands. Tafari desperately threw the empty rocket launcher at

Tarzan, which he easily batted aside. Tafari drew his pistol and knew he only had one chance because his target was moving too fast.

Tarzan leapt as the gun report boomed and a bullet tore into his arm.

• • •

Keeping to the trees, Jane led the wary prisoners from confinement. They kept behind the cover of the trees and were guided by two black-back gorillas from Kerchak's clan, who they eyed with respect and caution.

Clark and Archie carried Robbie between them and glanced at the battle. For the first time they saw Tarzan as he burst from the flames and was shot in the arm.

"Oh my God!" spluttered Clark as he saw their savior crumple to his knees.

Mister David and Esmée brought up the rear and watched with distress as Tafari took aim for the final execution. They were so trans-fixed they couldn't stop Jane from bolting between them, out into the camp.

"NO!"

• • •

Jane's voice made Tafari hesitate for a fraction of a second as he glanced up to see his prisoners were escaping. But he didn't need to look to squeeze the trigger.

The shadows shifted and a dark feline shape sped toward Tafari—it was Sheeta. The panther's jaws were a blur as they sliced into Tafari's arm, forcing him to drop the gun before he could pull the trigger. He shrieked, dropping to his knees as he gripped his lacerated arm. The panther bounded away, across the clearing.

Tarzan sprang for Tafari, pinning him to the floor. The general used his one good hand to prevent Tarzan from strangling him. Tarzan's teeth gnashed close to Tafari's face, inches from taking a bite. Tafari concentrated all his strength on holding him back, but blood loss was making him weak.

Unable to bite him, Tarzan shifted his weight and went for Tafari's chest. Tafari levered his knee into Tarzan's stomach and pushed him off.

Tarzan rolled across the floor—giving Tafari a chance to snatch his fallen gun. He swung it at Tarzan—victory was certain . . .

Then he noticed Tarzan had three metal rings in his mouth.

Tarzan had seen man's violence and petty wars from across the jungle. He had witnessed the creative methods of killing they employed against each other. He had seen the destructive force of a grenade.

Tafari's hand patted the three grenades he had tied to his bandolier. The pins were missing!

Tarzan leapt for cover as Tafari exploded. Jane averted her gaze from the rebel's gory end. She ran across to where Tarzan had fallen.

"Tarzan?" Her heart was in her mouth when she saw he was sprawled in the mud. "No!" she sobbed, kneeling at his side. He surely couldn't be dead?

Then she noticed his chest heave, and Tarzan rolled over, shaking from his head the cloudy feeling caused by the explosion. He stood, hand clamped across the bullet in his arm, and looked at Jane. There was no victorious smile, just a calm expression as he assured himself that Jane was unhurt.

Around the camp, the last of the rebels perished with their weapons in hand. The others had fled into the trees only then to face the more deadly challenges of survival.

Tarzan raised his head to the sky and bellowed a victory cry that echoed across the jungle for everyone, and everything, to hear.

EPILOGUE

Tarzan had refused medical aid from Archie and dealt with the bullet wound himself. His army of beasts had melted into the jungle, save Tantor and his herd, who carried the weary loggers back to their own camp. At Tarzan's insistence, they had left the dead—human and animal—where they had fallen.

Tarzan and Jane rode Tantor. Tarzan never once acknowledged the constant stream of gratitude the loggers offered for saving their lives.

Fighting off fatigue, Jane spoke about the new life that awaited Tarzan.

"You are the heir to the Greystoke legacy. You don't belong out here. You have a home back in Britain." The words had no impact on Tarzan. Jane persisted. "There are people who want to know you are alive. Your parents were rich, very rich. Do you understand money?"

Tarzan shook his head. Jane sighed. How could she explain the importance of money to somebody who'd never heard of it? "You give money, I give you food."

Tarzan frowned. "Tarzan take food when hungry."

"No . . . look. You can buy a really nice home with lots of money."

"Tarzan has home."

Jane gave up. Wealth and status were meaningless to him. But surely it was important? Why else would people crave it? She wondered just who was waiting to hear news that Lord Greystoke's heir was alive and well. She would try to find out.

Back at the remains of Karibu Mji, Clark kicked the charred debris. Nothing had been spared save the bulldozer. The morning light added little cheer to the scene—their dreams were shattered, but at least they were alive.

"Now what do we do?" asked Jane as she looked around the ruins.

Archie shrugged. "I don't know."

Clark spoke up. He was already thinking ahead. "We carry on."

Jane was horrified, especially after everything they had just been through. "You can't do that! This is Tarzan's land!"

"Then we cut him in on the deal."

She pleaded with Archie, but her father could offer nothing other than a shrug.

Jane spun round to face Robbie, who was using a branch as a crutch. He looked wan, but insisted on walking despite Archie's warnings that he needed to get to a hospital quickly.

"Robbie, tell them!" Jane insisted.

"Tell them what? This was our plan, Jane, our dream. We can't just throw it away. Where else are we going to go?"

"Rob . . . you don't have to run. Not any more." He looked away, the shame of his actions shadowing his face. "You think you killed your stepfather, but he's still alive."

Robbie looked at her in astonishment. "How do you know that?"

Archie and Clark exchanged alarmed looks—Robbie's past was news to them.

Jane smiled gently. "You make a wonderful hero, and I'm glad to say, a terrible murderer. It's all over the Internet. You knocked him out and cracked his skull, but he's alive."

Robbie reeled from the implications. "The police still want you, but . . . it's not as bad as you think."

He wasn't a murderer! Even with every fiber of his being screaming with pain, Robbie managed a smile. It was a weight off his shoulders. However, it also meant the man responsible for his sister's death was still alive.

Jane turned back to Archie and Clark. "I researched some stuff on the Internet . . ."

Clark snorted. "Last time your dad did that, it nearly got us killed."

Jane ignored him. "Tarzan's really the son of Lord Greystoke. He has a whole legacy waiting for him! He was set to inherit a fortune. You have to listen to what he has to say."

She didn't see the greedy glance Clark gave to Archie.

Jane turned to find Tarzan. Even with his limited communication skills, he should be able to persuade them to see sense.

But Tarzan had vanished. Jane stared into the trees.

"He didn't even say goodbye," she whispered.

Robbie leaned on her shoulder. "We owe him, Jane. We really do. But I think the fact that he's not here tells you he doesn't care what we do. He doesn't understand." Robbie laughed. "The guy thinks his mother was an ape!"

Jane didn't tear her gaze from the trees. Tarzan was out there somewhere. She knew she hadn't seen the last of him.

ACKNOWLEDGMENTS

Being able to follow in the illustrious footsteps of Edgar Rice Burroughs was a huge privilege and I would like to thank James Sullos, Cathy Wilbanks, and everybody at ERB for trusting me with their most prized possession.

Bristol Zoo (www.bristolzoo.org.uk) provided endless support in research, so thank you to Lizy Jones, Dr. Bryan Carroll, Simon Robinson, and John Partridge for all your time and research advice—any inaccuracies are entirely my own fault!

A big thank you to Julian and Eva for your sterling work on something that turned out so complex; PR whizz Kate Adamson for creating waves; and the wonderful Lindsey Heaven and Elv Moody for kick-starting me on my journey.

Finally, a huge Tarzan yodel to Julia Heydon-Wells and everybody at Faber who turned this all into a reality.

For those of you I left out, you are not forgotten!

ONE HUNDRED YEARS
OF TARZAN

EDGAR RICE BURROUGHS
AND TARZAN

From the day he was born in Chicago, on September 1, 1875, until he submitted half of a novel to *All-Story Magazine* in 1911, Edgar Rice Burroughs failed in nearly every enterprise he tried.

He attended half a dozen public and private schools before he finally graduated in 1895 from Michigan Military Academy, an institution he described as "a polite reform school."

Having failed the entrance examination for the United States Military Academy at West Point, he enlisted as a private in the Seventh US Cavalry because he thought he might still obtain a commission as an officer if he distinguished himself in a different assignment. He asked to be sent to the worst post in America—a request the authorities speedily granted.

The post was Fort Grant in the Arizona desert, and his mission, as he put it, was to "chase outlaw Apaches." "I chased a good many Apaches," he said, "but fortunately for me, I never caught up with any of them."

Private Burroughs soon had his fill of Fort Grant, and after one year he was discharged. In 1900, he married Emma Centennia Hulbert, who dutifully followed him back and forth across America during the next eleven years.

He became a cowboy in Idaho, then a shopkeeper, a railroad policeman, a gold miner, and even an "expert accountant," although he knew nothing of the profession. Throughout this period he somehow raised money for a number of his own businesses, all of which sank without a trace.

Life was dismal for the newly married couple. Burroughs became depressed; his wife, discouraged. Perhaps to escape from the grim reality of their lives, or perhaps to amuse Emma, he would often sketch darkly humorous cartoons or write fantastic fairy tales.

By 1911, Burroughs's position had become so desperate that not even his cartoons and stories could block out the frustrating fact of his successive failures. He even went so far as to apply for a commission in the Chinese army. (The application was summarily rejected.) He also applied for a post with Teddy Roosevelt's Rough Riders, but there were no vacancies.

Finally he reached rock bottom. He was thirty-five years old, without a job, without money. In addition to his wife and two children, a third child was expected soon. He could buy food and coal only by pawning his watch and Emma's jewelry.

While working as a manager for pencil-sharpener salesmen, he used his leisure moments while "waiting for them to come back to tell me that they had not sold any," to begin writing *Under the Moons of Mars*, his first story. He recalled:

> I had no idea how to submit a story or what I could expect in payment. Had I known anything about it at all, I would never have thought of submitting half a novel, but that is what I did. Thomas Newell Metcalf, then editor of *All-Story Magazine* . . . wrote me that he liked the first half of the story and if the second was as good he thought he might use it. Had he not given me this encouragement, I would never have finished the story and my writing career would have been at an end, since I was not writing because of any urge to write nor for any particular love of writing. I was writing because I had a wife and two babies, a combination which does not work well without money.

I finished the second half of the story and got $400 for first magazine serial rights. The check was the first big event in my life. No amount of money today could possibly give me the thrill that this first $400 check gave me.

Today, scholars consider that story to be the turning point of twentieth-century science fiction. New editions continue to be published annually throughout the world.

But Burroughs was still a long way from becoming an established writer. His next literary effort, a historical novel set in the England of the Plantagenet kings, was rejected. He nearly gave up but his publisher would not hear of it. "Try again," the publisher urged. "Stick with the 'damphool' stuff."

Burroughs did, and with his next novel, his future was decided. The novel was *Tarzan of the Apes*. An astonishing success on its appearance in *All-Story Magazine* in 1912, *Tarzan of the Apes* brought Edgar Rice Burroughs $700 and a surge of success. Burroughs sent the manuscript to book publishers but was rejected by practically every major company in the country. Finally, *Tarzan* was printed as a novel from A.C. McClurg and Co., and it became a bestseller in 1914.

Said Burroughs, "In all these years I have not learned one single rule for writing fiction. I still write as I did thirty years ago; stories which I feel would entertain me and give me mental relaxation, knowing that there are millions of people just like me who will like the same things I like. Anyway, I have great fun with my imaginings, and I can appreciate—in a small way—the swell time God had in creating the universe."

A torrent of novels followed *Tarzan*: stories about Mars, Venus, Apaches; Westerns; social commentaries; detective stories; tales of the Moon and of a fictional Hollow Earth—and more and more Tarzan books. By the time his pen was stilled, nearly one hundred stories bore Edgar Rice Burroughs's name.

In 1918, Tarzan debuted on screen in the silent film *Tarzan of the Apes*, starring Elmo Lincoln. It became one of the first films in history to earn one million dollars. Since then, fifty Tarzan live-action films, 115 one-hour television episodes, seventy-one half-hour animated television episodes, and three feature animation films have been produced, with more than twenty-seven actors playing the lead role.

Although he joked about the films, Burroughs was bitterly disappointed with the Tarzan motion pictures. Often he would not go to see them. His Tarzan was a supremely intelligent, sensitive man. His Tarzan sat in the House of Lords when not otherwise occupied in the upper terraces of the African jungle. His Tarzan was a truly civilized man—heroic, handsome, and above all, free.

In 1919, with financial security assured, Burroughs moved to California, where he purchased the 550-acre estate of General Harrison Gray Otis, renaming it "Tarzana Ranch." By 1923, the city of Los Angeles had completely surrounded Tarzana Ranch, and Burroughs sold a large portion of it for home sites. In 1930, a post office was established, and the three hundred residents held a contest to find a name for the new community. The winning entry was "Tarzana."

By the mid-1930s, daily and special Sunday Tarzan comic strips appeared in more than 250 newspapers all over the world. Tarzan radio serials thrilled millions of listeners across the country, with Burroughs's daughter, Joan, in the role of Jane, and her husband, James H. Pierce—who had played the lead in the silent movie *Tarzan and the Lion Men*—as Tarzan.

Today, Tarzan television programs and films are shown on an array of different networks all over the world. A Tarzan movie plays somewhere in the world every day. And with the contemporary emphasis on outer space, Burroughs's science fiction writings are still treasured.

In 1942, Burroughs became America's oldest war correspondent, covering stories with the Pacific Fleet for United Press. He returned home from the South Pacific only after suffering a series of heart attacks. Ironically, he was unable to find a suitable home in Tarzana, and he spent his remaining years in a modest house in nearby Encino. It was there, on March 19, 1950, that he set down his pen for the final time.

The last line he ever wrote:

"Thank God for everything."

Burroughs around age ten.

Edgar Rice Burroughs at age sixteen in Idaho.

Burroughs's friends and fellow soldiers, known as "the May-have-seen-
better-days Club," at Fort Grant, Arizona, in 1896.

Tarzan of the Apes (1918), a silent film, was the first Tarzan movie ever made and one of the first movies to ever earn one million dollars. The success of the film allowed Burroughs to buy the ranch he named Tarzana.

In 1919, Burroughs purchased a ranch near Los Angeles with the money he earned from the first Tarzan movie, calling the property "Tarzana." As the city spread around the ranch, Burroughs sold part of it for development, and in 1930, his neighbors voted to name their new town Tarzana.

In 1922, Burroughs's old friend, Robert D. Lay from the Michigan Military Academy, visited Burroughs's California ranch. Lay had become president of a large life insurance company.

Buster Crabbe, an Olympic swimmer, stepped into the title role for 1933's *Tarzan the Fearless*, opposite Jacqueline Wells.

Burroughs reviewing *Tarzan and the Lion Man*, the seventeenth book in the series, in 1934. *Lion Man* is the closest thing to a comic novel in the Tarzan series, with Burroughs satirizing Hollywood's treatment of the Tarzan character and even spoofing his own work

Burroughs dictating into an Ediphone in March 1937.

Burroughs, right, and Cyril Ralph Rothmund, his secretary and manager for many years, in 1937.

Burroughs working on a story at his Honolulu office on November 21, 1941. He wrote many stories in this office, and sent them to his secretary-manager, Rothmund, in Tarzana. Rothmund then arranged for retyping and submission to magazine editors.

Johnny Weissmuller and Maureen O'Sullivan costarred
in many of the Tarzan films.

Burroughs with his grandchildren, John Ralston Burroughs, James
Michael Pierce, and Danton Burroughs, in 1945.

Burroughs with Lex Barker, the tenth movie Tarzan.

Since 1912, the Tarzan character has been brought to life in television, movies, newspaper comic strips, comic books, and art. Illustrator Frank Frazetta began creating cover art for Burroughs's Tarzan paperbacks in the 1960s, a period when Frazetta's work was redefining fantasy art.

TARZAN: A TWENTY-FIRST-CENTURY LEGEND

The year 2012 sees the centenary of an iconic figure. One hundred years ago Tarzan first swung from the jungle and into the pages of *All-Story Magazine*. Through books, comics, films, radio shows, and countless television shows, Tarzan left an indelible mark on the public's imagination. Generations still know who he is even if they've never read one of Edgar Rice Burroughs's twenty-six original Tarzan novels. There is no better time than the one-hundred-year anniversary to give new life to the world's first eco-warrior.

To author Andy Briggs, it was clear that if somebody didn't inject new life into Tarzan, the character was in danger of eventually becoming extinct, consigned to pop-culture memory. But when he approached the Edgar Rice Burroughs estate to suggest Tarzan be reinvented for a whole new generation of readers, he was astonished by the estate's overwhelmingly enthusiastic response. They agreed it was time for a contemporary Tarzan.

With the estate's blessing, Briggs was given rein to bring Tarzan into the twenty-first century. Everything we know and love about the character has been maintained: He's still an English lord raised in the wild by apes, and he's often a wild untamable savage. But gone are the clichéd native tribes, replaced by warring rebel guerrillas. Jane is no longer an inactive damsel in distress; she's now a modern teenager who proves herself more than a match for the Lord of the Jungle. And Tarzan himself is not only Lord of the Jungle, but also a symbol for all that is good and noble, and for the preservation of the wild, untamable regions of our natural world.

Andy Briggs, author of the latest Tarzan books.

ANDY BRIGGS is a screenwriter, graphic novelist, and author. He has written for movie projects such as *Judge Dredd*, *Freddy vs. Jason*, and *Aquaman*. He also collaborated with *Spider-Man* creator Stan Lee and legendary producer Robert Evans on the screenplay for *Foreverman*. Briggs struck an eight-book deal with Oxford University Press for two series: Hero.com and Villain.net. His graphic novels include *Kong: King of Skull Island*, *Ritual*, and *Dinocorps*. He has recently rebooted the classic character Tarzan with his novels *Tarzan: The Greystoke Legacy* and *Tarzan: The Jungle Warrior*.

Trademark Tarzan owned by Edgar Rice Burroughs, Inc. and Used By Permission

The right of Andy Briggs and Edgar Rice Burroughs, Inc. to be identified as co-authors of this work has been asserted in accordance with Section 77 of the copyright, Designs & Patents Act of 1988

Cover design by the-parish.com and Andrea C. Uva

ISBN: 978-1-4532-7107-0

Published in 2012 by Open Road Integrated Media
180 Varick Street
New York, NY 10014
www.openroadmedia.com

Nov 13
J
Adventure

EBOOKS BY ANDY BRIGGS

FROM OPEN ROAD MEDIA

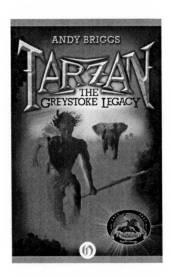 

Available wherever ebooks are sold

OPEN ROAD
INTEGRATED MEDIA

Open Road Integrated Media is a digital publisher and multimedia content company. Open Road creates connections between authors and their audiences by marketing its ebooks through a new proprietary online platform, which uses premium video content and social media.

Videos, Archival Documents, and New Releases

Sign up for the Open Road Media newsletter and get news delivered straight to your inbox.

Sign up now at
www.openroadmedia.com/newsletters

FIND OUT MORE AT
WWW.OPENROADMEDIA.COM

FOLLOW US:
@openroadmedia and
Facebook.com/OpenRoadMedia

CPSIA information can be obtained at www.ICGtesting.com
Printed in the USA
BVOW010012180912

300538BV00003B/1/P